P9-AFV-202

DATE DUE

JE 11 '95			
NO 5 '95			
AP 2 8 '95			
RENEW			
MT 5 '95			
JE 1 '95			
MY 5 '96			
NV 1			
JE 1 8 '99			
NO 2 2 '02			
JE 7 '02			

DEMCO 38-296

HOW
HAZARDOUS
SUBSTANCES
TOXIC THREAT
POISON
OUR
LIVES

STEPHEN J. ZIPKO

HOW
HAZARDOUS
SUBSTANCES
TOXIC THREAT
POISON
OUR
LIVES

JULIAN  MESSNER

Published by Julian Messner, a division of
Silver Burdett Press, Inc., Simon & Schuster, Inc.
Prentice Hall Bldg., Englewood Cliffs, NJ 07632.

JULIAN MESSNER and colophon are trademarks of
Simon & Schuster, Inc.
Design by Malle N. Whitaker

Manufactured in the United States of America.

Lib. ed.   10 9 8 7 6 5 4 3 2 1
Pbk. ed.   10 9 8 7 6 5 4 3 2 1

Library of Congress Cataloging-in-Publication Data

Zipko, Stephen James, 1948–
      Toxic Threat : how hazardous substances poison our lives
/ Stephen J. Zipko.—Rev. ed.
            p.   cm.
      Includes bibliographical references.
      Summary: Describes hazardous substances in our
environment, how they get there, and the problems they cause.
      1. Hazardous wastes—Environmental aspects—United
States—Juvenile literature.   2. Factory and trade waste—
Environmental aspects.—United States—Juvenile
literature.   [1. Hazardous wastes—Environmental—
Environmental aspects.   2. Factory and trade waste—
Environmental aspects.   3. Pollution.]   I. Title.
TD1040.Z56   1990
363.72'87—dc20   89-13790
ISBN 0-671-69330-1 (lib. bdg.)   CIP
ISBN 0-671-69331-X (pbk.)   AC

*This book is dedicated to my
mother who, like Mother Earth,
continues to sustain me with
her warmth and wisdom.*

CONTENTS

INTRODUCTION

In this century, many synthetic substances have been developed for the purpose of helping people lead a "good" life. As one result the life span of humans has greatly increased, and life has become more comfortable, thanks to the development of medicinal drugs, plastics, synthetic fibers, pesticides, and fertilizers. At the same time, most of these advances bring with them problems that are sometimes serious.

Thousands of synthetic substances are being used in the United States today. A great many of these have been found toxic. Many others have not been properly tested at all, and may or may not be toxic. Most of these synthetic substances are not water soluble, therefore they accumulate in the fatty tissues of organisms instead of passing through them. In the food chain or food web these substances become highly concentrated and can cause severe toxic effects in humans, who are on top of the food pyramid.

Toxic chemicals enter the human body not only by ingestion, but also by inhalation and absorption through the skin. Pesticides on fruits and vegetables, black smoke from a truck's diesel engine, polluted water used for bathing are all sources of toxics for humans. For toxic substances, the low-concentration, long-term exposure health effects are not yet known.

Some people may argue that technological and engineering methods have caused the environmental problems and that scientists will inevitably solve them. Not so. Our environmental problems can be solved only if all people, not just the experts, work together. Everybody talks about hazardous wastes, but now you can be informed and can do something about them. Radio, television, and newspapers report about the threat of toxic chemicals in our environment. To be an active participant in our democratic society, to speak up or to write to your congressman or even to the President, you must be familiar with the subject matter or you will not be taken seriously. This book will give you a good introduction to the subject. It will teach you and encourage you to do your own investigation and critical thinking in reference to problems and solutions. Stephen Zipko's *Toxic Threat* will tell you how.

Frances S. Sterrett, Ph.D.
Environmental Chemist
Hofstra University
Long Island, New York

PREFACE

This book is about the problems that humans have created in the environment we all share. While you are reading this, many pounds of hazardous chemical wastes are finding their way into our water, land, and air. These wastes are discarded from factories, towns, perhaps even from your own home. The problems related to the disposal of this waste have grown in recent years.

As a nation, we are using more materials every year, including hazardous substances. These toxics are used all around us. The wastes from these materials go up smokestacks to foul the air, or they go into rivers to pollute the water and land. We have not begun to manage properly the enormous problem they are creating.

In this book we will explore what makes a substance hazardous, how these materials affect natural cycles, and how we can decide whether the benefits they give us are worth the danger involved. We will look at how hazardous wastes are handled and how these processes need to be changed to lower our risks.

Throughout the book you will find activities and experiments that explore the actions of hazardous substances. As you try them out, think of the effects that these materials have on a large scale on our environment. Record all of your experiment results in a notebook for later study. As you become more aware of hazards in your air, water, and food, you will be interested in following what industry and government are doing to solve this important problem.

HOW
HAZARDOUS
SUBSTANCES
TOXIC THREAT
POISON
OUR
LIVES

CHAPTER 1:
PROBLEMS WITH NATURAL CYCLES

Our planet has a limited supply of natural resources. These resources include substances found in soil, air, and water. The earth does not get more water, air, or minerals from outer space. We can use only what is here now.

Because we have a fixed amount of natural resources, they must move in cycles between the water, air, and soil. They go through the bodies of living things and through soil and rain, and back again to their source. As dead things decay, substances are put back into the soil. There they act as nutrients to aid plant growth. Plants, of course, serve as food for animals. By interfering with plant life, we can hinder nature in its natural recycling process.

THE WATER CYCLE

First, consider the natural process that circulates water between the oceans, air, and land. This process is called the *water cycle*. After rain falls on the earth's surface, the water follows one of several paths. Part of it flows over the land to streams or lakes, then back to the ocean. From there it evaporates back to the air.

Transpiration is an important part of the water cycle. During transpiration, plants take up water from the soil through their roots and give it up again through their leaves.

Some water is pulled by gravity into the ground. This is called *groundwater*. Many people use either surface water from reservoirs or groundwater from wells for drinking, cooking, and bathing.

Water is an excellent solvent. Drinking water contains minerals that give it taste. Yet water can also have large amounts of toxic chemicals dissolved in it. These chemicals are added by factories, businesses, even private citizens. Many such chemicals are carried down through several soil layers to where groundwater is stored.

Sometimes groundwater forms underground lakes. But often it moves several yards a day, both downward and sideways, if the material below the topsoil is sand and gravel. (Water cannot easily seep through clay. In clay soil, the water may move only half an inch a day.) Wherever sand and gravel lie below the topsoil, groundwater—and many of the chemicals it carries—may travel deep below the surface. It may also travel hundreds of miles from where it entered the ground. Such underground systems of moving water trapped between layers of soil, gravel, or rock are called *aquifers*.

Aquifers are complex underground channel systems

that move very slowly. Each main channel sends out branches, often in many directions. Thus, chemicals in an aquifer are hard to track because they can flow in any of several directions, depending on the grade or angle of the bedrock.

THE NITROGEN CYCLE

Nitrogen follows another natural cycle. As it exists in the air, nitrogen cannot be used by living things for growth and repair of cells. It must be changed to other forms by soil bacteria before it can be used. Once changed by these organisms into a water-soluble form, nitrogen can be used by living organisms for making nutrients such as proteins. After the organisms die, they decay. Some of the decay-causing bacteria and fungi change the nitrogen-containing matter back to elemental nitrogen, which is released into the atmosphere again.

Humans interfere with the nitrogen cycle by producing large amounts of nitrogen oxide gas in auto exhausts and factory smokestacks. Nitrogen and oxygen form the gas in the air at very high temperatures.

This nitrogen oxide upsets the nitrogen cycle by combining with water vapor in the air to form nitric acid. Some of this nitric acid is washed out of the atmosphere during rainfall and falls to the ground as acid rain. The acid rain is absorbed by plants and can harm them and the animals that eat them. Nitrogen oxide can also combine with the sun's ultraviolet radiation to form ozone and smog. Both ozone and smog can cause the eyes to burn and can damage crops.

Today we use large amounts of synthetic fertilizers to grow crops. Such synthetic fertilizers contain nitrates, chemicals containing nitrogen. This nitrogen can harm the fish and other animals in streams and rivers by upsetting the ecosystem.

Algae in the water use sunlight to form oxygen through photosynthesis. When excessive amounts of nitrates wash off farmland into streams, too many algae grow in the water because nitrogen is a nutrient for them. When the algae become too abundant (bloom) they begin to die off because they themselves cut off the sunlight they need. The increase of dead algae leads to an increase in the decomposing organisms because they have ample food supply. These organisms consume the oxygen from the water, causing the death of many stream animals. Nitrates can also seep directly into groundwater and contaminate it.

THE PHOSPHORUS CYCLE

Phosphorus is vital to all living things. It provides them with energy, and is essential for all living cells. Normally, phosphorus is present as phosphate in certain types of rock. It is usually made available to plants only as natural erosion or earthquakes break down rocks. Some of the phosphates released by erosion of phosphate rocks pass through plants and animals on their way to the ocean.

This occurs when phosphate rock is dissolved in water that passes through the soil. Plant roots absorb phosphate, which is a nutrient, just like nitrate. When the animals eat the plants, the phosphorus is passed on to them. When they die, phosphorus eventually returns to the soil, rivers, and oceans as their bodies decay. But since this takes time, humans mine phosphorus-bearing rock from deep underground caverns.

The mined phosphorus is mixed with nitrate during the production of synthetic fertilizers. The main elements needed by plants for growth are carbon, hydrogen, oxygen, potassium, phosphorus, and nitrogen. The three numbers on a fertilizer bag stand for nitrogen, phosphorus, and potassium.

Excessive use of phosphorus in fertilizer causes a rapid increase of phosphorus in streams and lakes. The limiting factor for growth is almost always the nutrient that contains phosphorus. If phosphorus is plentiful, excessive algal growth occurs. Phosphorus thus contributes to the overgrowth of stream algae. As these algae die and decay, the oxygen level in the stream drops, causing some freshwater fish to die.

THE CARBON CYCLE

Carbon is another important element in cells. Green plants use solar energy to combine carbon dioxide with water to form such substances as sugars and oxygen during photosynthesis. Most land plants get carbon from the carbon dioxide in the atmosphere. The ocean's plants get their carbon from dissolved carbon dioxide.

Animals combine these sugars with oxygen to produce carbon dioxide, water, and heat energy during respiration. Green plants use this carbon dioxide. Respiration and photosynthesis are opposite chemical and physical processes. The two processes operate together as a closed cycle through which plants produce oxygen used by animals and absorb the carbon dioxide given off by animals.

Another source of carbon is the burning of fossil fuel, which releases carbon into the air. Heavy use of carbon-containing fossil fuels (coal, oil, and natural gas) began over one hundred years ago. Human activities since then seem to be unbalancing the carbon cycle. An extra 6 billion tons of carbon dioxide are added to the atmosphere each year when fuels are burned. Another 2 billion tons enter the atmosphere each year when fields are plowed, because plowing releases carbon dioxide that would otherwise have stayed in the soil. The rapid cutting of forests also may be increasing the amount of carbon by removing the trees that use carbon dioxide.

Moreover, we are burning carbon-containing fuels at increasing rates. This growth is expected to pump more carbon dioxide into the atmosphere. Carbon dioxide absorbs much solar heat. Excess carbon dioxide in the atmosphere traps more heat close to the earth's surface, thus increasing global temperatures. The National Academy of Sciences estimates that average global temperatures will rise by 2 to 8° Fahrenheit (1 to 3.5° Celsius) over the next fifty to one hundred years.

FOOD CHAINS AND WEBS

In addition to these natural cycles, there also exist millions of food chains. Creatures in a food chain generally feed only on one or a few species. They are in turn hunted by one or a few other species. Food chains are simplest and contain the least number of links in those places where conditions are harshest. Such a place is the Arctic tundra. One Arctic food chain is made up of a few plants that are eaten by caribou, which are in turn eaten by wolves.

A food chain shows only one kind of food for each organism along the way. In real life, however, people and other animals eat several kinds of food. They are part of many different food chains. These chains are all connected to one another in a *food web*.

Humans can damage food webs in many different ways. Using insecticides, like DDT, is one way. The discovery of DDT made it possible to control mosquitoes that carry malaria. It is still used for that purpose. Some pests destroyed crops around the world. DDT could protect crops in hungry nations.

Then we discovered some alarming news about DDT. We found that it stays around for a long time. It travels a long way through many complex food webs. DDT has shown up in the bodies of penguins in Antarctica, where no spraying has ever been done. It has also been found in the eggshells of eagles, hawks, and other birds of prey. Young salmon died from too much DDT in their egg sacs. DDT does not dissolve in water, but does dissolve readily in fats. Thus, it can be concentrated in the fatty tissue of animals and accumulated or magnified as smaller animals are eaten by larger ones. This process is called *biomagnification.*

What do penguins, eagles, hawks, and salmon have in common? They all occupy the top steps of food chains. The closer an organism is to the top of a food chain, the more likely it is to contain large amounts of fat-soluble insecticides.

In the waters of Long Island Sound, for example, only 0.000003 parts per million (ppm) of DDT were found. But let's follow DDT through the food chain—from plankton, to small fish, to large fish, and finally to fish-eating birds. The birds eat several large fish. These large fish have eaten many small fish. These small fish have eaten thousands of tiny plankton. Thus the birds are getting nearly all the DDT that the tiny organisms ate, a whopping 25 ppm!

Since we human beings are at the top of the food web, we also get a large dose of DDT from the foods we eat. How it will affect us in the long run, we do not yet know. But the effects of DDT on animals were damaging enough. Such effects convinced a court in the early 1970s that DDT ought to be banned in this country. It would be used only in extreme cases. DDT is still used in some other nations, mostly to control malaria. A variety of other insecticides are still being used in this country.

Synthetic organic substances, especially chlorinated hydrocarbons like DDT, are foreign to nature, and will biomagnify. Biomagnification in food chains occurs only if three factors are present. First is the general fact about food chains that so little energy gets shifted from one link to the next. Thus, a small fish must eat lots of plankton to survive. Larger fish must eat lots of small fish to live. And a pelican has to eat many larger fish to live.

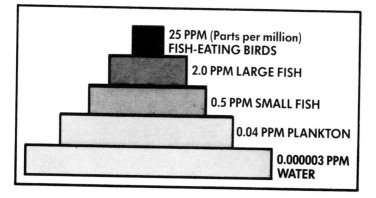

25 PPM (Parts per million)
FISH-EATING BIRDS

2.0 PPM LARGE FISH

0.5 PPM SMALL FISH

0.04 PPM PLANKTON

0.000003 PPM
WATER

The concentration of DDT is biomagnified 10 million times in a food chain on Long Island Sound.

In order for chemicals to biomagnify, they must be soluble (dissolvable) in fat but not in water. DDT is fat soluble, but water insoluble. Let's say each plankton concentrates one unit of DDT from the water. Then a small fish eating thousands of plankton will store thousands of units of DDT in its fat cells. If DDT were water soluble, like sugar, the fish would get rid of it by elimination at each link of the food chain.

The third factor in biomagnification is that the breakdown or decomposition of the chemicals is so slow that they remain in the environment for a long time. Many synthetic chemicals, like DDT, meet this requirement. Anything that is not degraded or removed from the environment as that substance moves through the food chain or food web will become more concentrated as it accumulates in the fat of an organism.

In this chapter we have seen how natural cycles, food chains, or food webs should operate. They are delicately balanced and easily upset by hazardous substances produced by humans. Through biomagnification, tiny amounts of toxic substances can disrupt food chains and webs.

EXPERIMENTS

Recycling Matter in Nature

In this investigation you will set up three experiments that will allow you to observe the recycling of water, organic matter, and air.

You will need two large clear plastic bags, garden soil, a potted plant (such as a geranium), a sprig of a vine (such as ivy), tape, a large glass jar, a fresh-picked leaf, and some water.

A. Water Cycle

Water the potted plant and cover it with a clear plastic bag. Be sure to seal the bag around the top of the pot. Place the pot in a well-lighted area.

Observe it carefully for the next day or two. What do you notice on the inside of the plastic? Where is this matter coming from? What cycle does this demonstrate, and why is this cycle important?

B. Organic Matter Decay

Place 5 to 10 centimeters of soil in the glass jar. Put a plant leaf on top of the soil, and add some water.

Keep the jar in a warm location. Moisten the contents every few days. Keep a record of any changes in the leaf you observe during the next few weeks. What is happening to the leaf? How does this affect the environment? What cycle is demonstrated, and why is it important?

C. Carbon Cycle

Place 5 centimeters of soil in a plastic bag. Plant a small sprig of ivy or another vine in the bag by placing the cut end of the vine into the soil. Water the plant.

Tie a knot at the top of the bag so that it is sealed. Place the bag in a well-lighted area.

Observe the changes in the plant over the next two weeks. Do not add any more water. Does the ivy continue to live and grow? If so, how does it survive without a constant fresh supply of oxygen? Where does the plant get the carbon dioxide it needs to make food?

In your notebook, describe how each of your three experiments is similar to the way matter is recycled in the environment.

CHAPTER 2:
WHEN IS A SUBSTANCE HAZARDOUS?

While reading the last chapter, you may have wondered: at what point does DDT become deadly? At what level is it only mildly harmful? What kind of harm does it cause? At what point is it not harmful at all? And the big question: how do you tell the difference between these levels?

This is a chemical world. Human beings as well as animals and plants consist of chemicals. The air we breathe, the water we drink, the foods we eat, all consist of chemicals. Many substances are hazardous at high-dose levels. It is the dose that makes a chemical either harmless or harmful. Ten times the normal dose of aspirin, for example, can be harmful. So can forty times the normal level of vitamin A. Small doses of some chemicals taken frequently are just as bad as large doses of other substances taken only once.

Yet people live with dangerous chemicals every day. They can do this because they are careful not to exceed their limits of tolerance. Scientists call this the *principle of acceptable risk.*

TOXICITY VERSUS HAZARD

Toxicity is the ability of a chemical to cause injury to an organism. The injury may be caused by the chemical itself or by substances formed when the chemical is changed inside the body.

Each plant or animal has its own response to a chemical. A certain dose of a substance may be deadly to rabbits. The same dose may have a lesser effect on rats or dogs.

The effects brought about by a chemical depend on many circumstances, including age, sex, species, dose level, and frequency of dose or exposure. The effects may also depend on how rapidly the organism gets rid of the substance, and on the chemical nature of the new compounds produced by the body as it reacts to the substance.

To find out how hazardous a substance can be, scientists must learn its effects. Only then can they recommend how to use and store the chemical properly.

EXPOSURE AND RESPONSE

There is a no-effect level for almost any material. This is the highest dose or exposure that causes no ill effects. Injury is unlikely if people or animals are exposed to amounts of a chemical below this level.

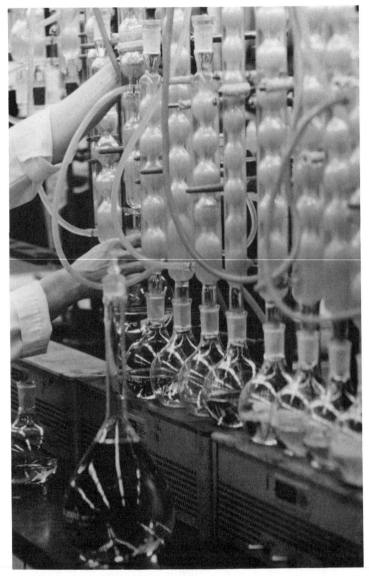

Elaborate laboratory equipment is used to test water for toxic chemicals.

Photo courtesy W.R. Grace Company

The *toxicity threshold* is the lowest dose level at which toxic effects are seen. Toxicology is the science that deals with poisons and their effects. Its aim is to find out the toxic thresholds of chemicals. Researchers then work backward to find the no-effect level.

To do this, they run various lab tests. The nature of each test depends on the intended use of the chemical. Using rabbits, rats, or mice, scientists perform tests to learn the effects of (1) swallowing a chemical, (2) splashing it on the skin, (3) splashing it into the eyes, or (4) breathing it as a vapor, mist, or dust.

Each of these four tests can be made with different doses. They can likewise be done for different time periods. Some tests last from several hours to days, and are done at the highest doses. From these tests, scientists can learn how rapidly an injury can occur.

Other tests last about ninety days. They give scientists more data about the effects of repeated exposure or multiple doses of a substance. Blood and tissue samples are taken often from test animals during this period. Scientists can thus track the changes in the animal's body and blood.

Still other tests last about two years, sometimes three. This is the life span of most laboratory rats and mice. Small doses of a chemical are given continuously as the animals age. Most of these tests are done to learn if a chemical is a *carcinogen* (causes cancer). Other tests determine if the chemical is a *mutagen* (causes mutations, or changes in the genetic material inside cells) or a *teratogen* (causes birth defects).

Experiments on lab animals are expensive. Rodent

studies may cost millions of dollars. Yet each test involves only several hundred test animals and untreated control animals. Several years of tests are needed to produce meaningful results.

TESTING FOR CARCINOGENS

Because there may be a long time between exposure and visible signs of cancer, many scientists see the need for better tests than those described above. The big problem is how to identify carcinogens before they enter our environment. We are trying to protect people. Yet we cannot experiment on humans directly. We can only do studies on groups who have long used a chemical, for example in the workplace. This method of matching disease in human groups with possible causes is called *epidemiology.* Such studies give data on chemical causes of diseases such as cancer, but only after that chemical has already caused human cancers.

Some 70,000 chemicals are made in industrial laboratories on a large scale today. Between 500 and 1,000 new ones are introduced each year. Most of the chemicals in commerce have not been completely tested in animals.

HOW MUCH IS A PART PER MILLION? BILLION? TRILLION?

Twenty years ago, science could measure only in parts per million (ppm). Impurities below that range could not be found. Now we can often detect impurities in parts per billion (ppb) or trillion (ppt). The result is that we are finding impurities more often in our food, water, and other products. These toxic substances can sometimes cause health problems at levels a person cannot detect with his or her own senses.

The question is, are these numbers so small that we can safely ignore them? Is 11 ppm of a toxic chemical in drinking water or air really a threat? How about 1 ppm? or 1 ppb?

The chemical industry might say we can ignore these numbers. Eleven parts per million is equal to an 11-ounce needle in a ton of hay or to eleven minutes in two years. These levels sound harmless. Also, some say that any dangers of toxic chemicals at such levels are outweighed by their potential or actual benefits, especially if used as recommended.

Comparison of parts per million, billion, and trillion.

One part per million (ppm) is equal to:
   One bottle of soda in a row of bottles over 40 miles long.
   One muffin in a stack of muffins 4 miles high.
   One car in a line of traffic 2,650 miles long.

One part per billion (ppb) is equal to:
   One cheeseburger in a chain of cheeseburgers circling the earth 2½ times.
   One step taken during a trip to the moon and back.
   One quarter in a stack of quarters nearly 1,500 miles high.

One part per trillion (ppt) is equal to:
   One minute of time in the past 1,920,000 years.
   One postage stamp in an area the size of Chicago.
   One six-inch "leap" on a 93-million-mile journey to the sun.

But let's look at this in another way. One part per million of a substance means there is 1 milligram of that chemical for every kilogram of water, soil, or body weight. For example, in an adult weighing 130 pounds, a dose of 1 ppm equals 59 milligrams.

Consider this in terms of a common aspirin tablet. The average aspirin tablet has 325 milligrams of active ingredient. Two tablets equal 650 milligrams, about 11 ppm in a 130-pound person. This dose of aspirin seems small. Yet it can stop pain and reduce fever. While 11 ppm may seem small, it can mean a lot of change in our bodies.

What, then, is considered safe? A chemical that might be carcinogenic at 100 ppm, but which is safe at 10 ppm? Where should we and the government draw the line? And based on whose evidence? For some toxic chemicals, a level of even 1 ppb or 1 ppt may be dangerous, especially for long-term exposure. There is no distinct threshold dose or safe concentration for many toxic substances.

SETTING STANDARDS

The federal government agency responsible for protecting our environment is the Environmental Protection Agency. The EPA is required to set levels, or standards, at which chemicals are believed to be safe. Since little is known about many chemicals, the EPA must run its own tests for toxicity. These animal tests must be repeated many times. Even after many tests, the results are not completely reliable, but the EPA must make a decision on standards for the chemical in question. If the agency decides to permit 5 ppm instead of 15 ppm, for instance, companies would have to purify the chemical further, at added cost.

For many years, environmentalists wanted the EPA to publish a list of toxic substances released by industry. Such a list was made public for the first time in 1989.

The list shows that 22.5 billion pounds of pollutants come from more than 74,000 industrial plants. About 9.6 billion pounds go into waterways; another 2.7 billion pounds are released into the air; 2.5 billion pounds are buried on land; and 3.2 billion pounds are injected into deep wells. The rest, 4.5 billion pounds, is treated before disposal. The EPA list tells us which industries released all these billions of pounds of more than 300 toxic chemicals. Only seven of these chemicals are now regulated by the EPA.

The EPA agrees that more control of these toxics is needed. The agency also says that you as a citizen have a right to know about the toxic material polluting your community. And you can find out by calling a toll-free number (1-800-535-0202) or by using a personal computer to gain access to the EPA's data base. We can now tell which polluters are poisoning the environment without ever having to set foot outside in that environment.

HOUSEHOLD CHEMICALS

Many household products are hazardous. When they are stored, used, or disposed of improperly, adults, children, and pets may be harmed.

But you don't have to endanger lives to clean your kitchen or garage. Certain chemicals require special care. You can learn how to identify hazardous products in your home and dispose of them properly. Reading the warnings on product labels will help you find out if something is reactive, corrosive, ignitable, or toxic.

Reactive products contain unstable compounds that react with other chemicals. They can explode or create poisonous gases when this occurs. Chlorine bleach mixed with ammonia or acid toilet bowl cleaner, for example, can form toxic gas.

Corrosives are very acid or alkaline products. They chemically eat away at substances. Corrosives can cause bad burns on contact. The vapors can burn the eyes. They are poisonous if swallowed. Examples include battery acid, drain openers, oven cleaners, chlorine bleach, and scouring powders.

Ignitable products pose a fire hazard. They irritate the skin, eyes, and lungs. They, too, emit harmful vapors and can be fatal if swallowed. Ignitable products include gasoline, paint, spot remover, and furniture polish.

Toxic products can poison living things, causing illness or death if swallowed. Many can also be absorbed through the skin. They include weed killers, insecticides, and household cleaners.

Some chemicals can react with their containers over the years. This causes the containers to decay. Disposing of these rusted, leaking cans could expose you to toxic substances.

When cleaning the garage or the kitchen, many people

dispose of several chemicals at the same time. This can be dangerous. Why? Because certain chemicals can react with each other and produce fumes or explode. This is also dangerous for garbage collectors; some of them have lost their sight or suffered eye problems when discarded chemicals were splattered. Exploding aerosol cans also cause many injuries.

Toxic substances can be hazardous to the environment. Used motor oil, for instance, is persistent and can contaminate groundwater. Never discard it with the rest of your garbage or pour it onto the ground. The best way to discard used motor oil is to put it in a plastic or glass bottle. Then take it to an agency that will recycle it.

RISK VERSUS BENEFIT

Earlier we referred to a policy called acceptable risk. Many chemical industry leaders have great faith in this policy. They would even accept the risk of some chemicals causing one or two cancers in a human population of, say, a million people. However, estimating human cancer risks is not accurate. Scientists cannot agree on the effect of low toxic doses in humans.

Can we not weigh the risks of a carcinogen against its benefits, instead of banning it? The idea is that a beneficial chemical should not be outlawed if it is only weakly carcinogenic.

Yet between 60 percent and 90 percent of human cancers are caused by substances in the environment, according to G. Tyler Miller's book *Living in the Environ-*

ment. Some environmental cancers are due to exposure to carcinogens at work. This includes radiation-caused cancers among workers at nuclear power plants, chemically caused cancers among workers in the oil and chemical industries, and asbestos-caused cancers in construction workers and those in the asbestos manufacturing industry.

Scientists in industry, government, and universities are doing research on toxic substances. The data they collect will help us to decide what the risks are, but again this will take time. Next, we must determine the benefits to be gained from use of the substances. Only then can people and government make intelligent choices about safety.

AN EXPERIMENT

Effects of Aspirin on Brine Shrimp

Obtain some brine shrimp from a pet store. Or your teacher can help you order them from a supplier. You will also need salt water made from 5 percent table salt in water, 4 paper cups, a lid from a glass jar, and aspirin tablets.

Fill 4 paper cups with equal amounts of salt water. (Brine shrimp normally live in salt water.) To prepare the aspirin solution, cut up two aspirin tablets. In one cup, place ¼ of a tablet and stir. Place ½ a tablet in the second cup and stir. Place one whole tablet in the third cup and stir. Do not place any aspirin in the last cup. This will be your control. Label each cup with the amount of aspirin in it. Label the last cup "normal behavior."

Now place two brine shrimp on the glass jar lid and drop them into the cup labeled "normal behavior." From the moment the shrimp are added, observe and record their behavior for five minutes. Does their behavior seem to change?

Place two other shrimp in the ¼-tablet cup. Record their behavior for five minutes. Do the same in the ½-tablet and whole-tablet cups. Record your findings in your notebook.

Which dose of aspirin stops brine shrimp motion most rapidly? Least rapidly? At which dose do you see the first signs of unusual behavior? What are these signs? Is such behavior definitely due to the chemical? What other circumstances might be causing it? How could you find out for sure?

Try the experiment again, using an aspirin substitute. See if the same results occur. If not, explain possible reasons.

CHAPTER 3:
WHAT ARE SYNTHETIC ORGANIC CHEMICALS?

Many hazardous substances are synthetic organic chemicals. These chemicals are not made by nature. They are manufactured by humans, using fossil fuels—coal, oil, and natural gas.

Fossil fuels are themselves formed from animal or plant remains by chemical reactions. When making new chemicals, scientists start with complex fossil fuel molecules. They treat them in different ways to produce the building blocks of many new substances we use every day. Many of these products are then treated further—with chlorine and other chemicals, for example. These compounds often do not occur in nature; they therefore resist decay, causing many of the environmental problems described later.

HOW ARE SYNTHETIC ORGANICS USED?

The total American production of synthetic organic chemicals increased from one billion pounds in 1940 to 350 billion in 1977. Why such fast growth? The answer is that we use these materials in so many ways.

Products made of synthetics have replaced many natural materials. Synthetics have also made possible the production of new products that cannot be made in large quantities from natural materials, because natural materials are not always abundant. So synthetics offer advantages to both the producer and consumer.

For example, atoms of chlorine can be added to certain molecules. This process produces some simple new compounds, like trichloroethylene (TCE) and perchloroethylene (PCE). These are industrial solvents. Many businesses use them to clean metal parts. PCE is used in dry cleaning, too.

The same atoms, put together in still other ways, can produce more complex organic chemicals. These include the insecticides DDT, mirex, and chlordane. Also included are herbicides, substances that kill plants, like 2,4-D and 2,4,5-T.

By adding chlorine to certain hydrocarbons, chemists make polychlorinated biphenyls (PCBs). By adding bromine instead of chlorine, they produce PBBs. Both of these have been useful chemicals.

WHAT ARE THE FEATURES OF SYNTHETIC ORGANICS?

The presence of chlorine and bromine in synthetic organic molecules makes the synthetics highly toxic. One special feature of these synthetic organic compounds is their persistence: they remain for a long time in the environment before decaying.

A second feature of synthetic organics is their insolubility in water. Try mixing a household insecticide with water. Unless it is already in suspension, in a liquid or a wettable powder, it will not totally dissolve. This trait increases the product's value for some purposes. It means the first rain will not wash the insecticides off the farmer's field. However, synthetic organics are much more soluble in fats. This, of course, makes them biomagnify easily.

Synthetic organics resist attack by the bacteria that decompose or break down dead organic materials. They slowly succumb to some decomposition but it may take as long as thirty years. An organism naturally tries to change certain chlorinated organic compounds or other toxic compounds present in its body. By doing so, the creature attempts to make the substance more water-soluble. But in doing this, often more toxic new compounds may be formed. An example is the fire ant insecticide mirex, which changes inside the ant to kepone, a deadly material.

WHAT ARE THE HAZARDS OF SYNTHETIC ORGANICS?

Useful as they are, synthetic organic chemicals can be hazardous. Acetone and chloroform, for example, are carcinogens (cancer-causing materials). Benzene causes anemia and leukemia, a form of cancer. Many synthetic insecticides are carcinogenic and cause poor reproduction in birds by weakening their eggshells. PCBs are carcinogenic and impair reproduction. PBBs are carcinogenic. Chlorinated dioxins are some of the most toxic chemicals. TCE, PCE, and carbon tetrachloride all produce cancer and birth defects in levels of only parts per trillion.

Many contaminants found in drinking water are toxic at high doses. Many of these affect the nervous system. They cause dizziness, nausea, poor coordination, blurred vision, lack of energy, and mental illness. Several cause kidney or liver damage. Some cause infertility, sterility, and chromosome damage.

At lower levels, some synthetic organics may produce acne and mildly affect the nervous system. And at still lower doses over many years they may cause cancer.

RISKS TO PUBLIC HEALTH

Many synthetic organic chemicals pose risks to our health in other ways; of the 70,000 in use today, most are hazardous. It is hard, however, to estimate the degree of, say, cancer risk from long-term exposure to low concentrations of any one of them. It is even harder to guess the risk from long exposure to combinations of them.

People living near synthetic-organic waste disposal sites are at high risk. The toxic substances at these sites may produce air pollution or seep into groundwater used for drinking.

A demonstration of the danger of living near a disposal site occurred when 40,000 abandoned steel drums exploded and burned at the Chemical Control disposal site in Elizabeth, New Jersey, in 1980. Toxic fumes carried synthetic organic chemicals known to cause nerve and blood damage, skin disorders, breathing problems, cancer, mutations, and birth defects. Schools were closed. Residents had to stay inside with closed windows. Scores of people were treated for nausea and irritation of throat, lungs, and eyes.

Transportation of synthetic organic wastes to dump sites also poses risks. Waste may be spilled in transit. Some transportation routes are known for their high rates of vehicle accidents. California state officials record one such spill or accident each day on their highways.

People who live or work in areas that are built on contaminated soil form a large risk group. As industries shut down, they too often leave toxic soil behind. Suppose houses, schools, or offices are built on that soil. Even in the distant future, heavy exposures may result, especially for children playing in or near the soil.

Some Synthetic Organic Chemicals and Their Effects.

CHEMICAL	LIMIT OF EXPOSURE	EFFECTS ON PEOPLE
Benzene	1–5 ppm	May cause cancer and mutations
Carbon tetrachloride	330 ppm	Affects nervous system, liver, kidneys
PCB	1 ppm	Known carcinogen
2,4-D	10 ppm	Causes mutations and birth defects
2,4,5-T	10 ppm	May cause mutations and birth defects; possible carcinogen
Dioxin	No safe level of exposure	Carcinogen mutagen
Toluene	200–500 ppm	Suspected carcinogen

THE LOVE CANAL EPISODE

Just such a situation occurred in Love Canal, a suburb of Niagara Falls, New York. Between 1947 and 1952, the Hooker Chemical and Plastics Corporation dumped over 21,000 tons of synthetic organic wastes into an old canal.

The scene at the Chemical Control Company explosion and fire in Elizabeth, New Jersey, in 1980. The steel drums contained toxic substances, and many of them were incorrectly labeled.

Photo, New Jersey Newsphotos

The wastes were stored in steel drums and the drums were covered with dirt.

In 1953, the company sold the canal area to the local school board for one dollar. An elementary school and several hundred homes were built on the land. Children played on the dump site.

From 1971 to 1977, heavy rains and snows made the place a muddy mess. Organic chemicals from the corroded barrels oozed into basements. The people complained to their city and county officials of various illnesses, but nothing was done for a long time. People living near the site had high levels of birth defects, miscarriages, kidney disorders, nerve ailments, breathing problems, and other illnesses.

In 1978, New York State spent $37 million moving 239 families away from the area. In 1980, President Carter declared the place a disaster area. He had the remaining people moved out at a cost of $30 million, relocating them in hotels, motels, and army barracks.

What about the Hooker Chemical Company? In 1979 the Justice Department filed a $124.5 million lawsuit against Hooker. In 1980 the New York State Attorney General filed a $635 million lawsuit against Hooker and its parent company. The company, however, says it sold the land to the school board only after the board threatened to condemn the area. Hooker also says the board built on the land after Hooker warned against it. The company says the dumping was legal at the time. It claims no proof exists connecting its chemicals with the ailments of Love Canal residents, and that its legal responsibility ceased when it sold the land.

Part of Love Canal, Niagara Falls, New York. The contaminated, filled-in canal was fenced off because of toxic chemicals coming to the surface and the presence of unsafe fumes.

Photo, AP/Wide World

In 1983, without admitting any negligence, the company made an out-of-court settlement for $20 million. By early 1985, the company still faced lawsuits from the state and federal governments, which wanted to recover the costs of cleaning up the area and relocating the people. In 1988, a Federal District Court found the parent company responsible for the cost of the cleanup begun in 1984. The cost was $250 million.

Meanwhile, because blood tests showed cell damage in 11 of 36 people, 710 more families had to be moved and the first of 227 homes was demolished in 1982. In 1983, the EPA found new chemical leaks in the area. The canal was covered over with a clay cap in 1984. The cleanup of the contaminated sewer system began in 1986. By 1987, the EPA had decided to burn all dioxin-contaminated soil taken from the site.

In 1988, the New York State Health Commissioner said that 250 abandoned houses could be lived in again, but another 250 could not be resettled due to chemical contamination.

The Love Canal episode reminds us that we can never really throw toxic materials away. They too often return, even if in some other form.

RISKS ON THE JOB

Workers in industries that produce or discard hazardous synthetics are at highest risk from exposure to these chemicals. About 2.5 million workers are exposed. Roughly 25 percent of industrial employees risk illness.

Love Canal, New York. The foundation remains where a house was removed to another location because of chemicals seeping into the basement. Houses in the background are boarded up and abandoned. The field between is part of the filled-in canal used as a chemical dump.

Photo, AP/Wide World

Love Canal, New York. A worker digging holes in the contaminated area. Water that seeped into the holes was tested for toxics.

Photo, AP/Wide World

Industry claims it has taken steps to protect workers. At least eighteen of our nation's largest companies are testing employees for genetic damage caused by chemicals they handle. Industry is likewise reducing exposure to proven toxins. According to *Hazardous Waste in America* by Samuel Epstein, Lester Brown, and Carl Pope, a recent study found that 88 percent of industries already had lowered limits on benzene exposure.

Yet in 1985, three company officials were found guilty of manslaughter in an employee's death from cyanide poisoning. The officials of a film treatment firm north of Chicago were held responsible for workplace conditions so unsafe that they led to the poisoning. The men were convicted of involuntary manslaughter, facing a fine of up to $10,000 and prison terms of twenty to forty years. This was the first case in which executives were held criminally responsible for an industrially related death.

IS THERE CAUSE FOR ALARM?

Prior to 1978, there was little public concern over hazardous substances. But after the Love Canal and Elizabeth, New Jersey, incidents, it increased. An ABC News-Harris Poll in 1980 found that 76 percent of the public considered the dumping of synthetic organics a serious problem. And 94 percent wanted government regulations against dumping to be more strict.

Is the public unduly alarmed? Federal officials do not think so, but some industries do. Different approaches to the problem must be found. Otherwise the problem will turn into a fight between industry and society.

Government response has been vigorous. But in many ways, as we shall see, it has failed to deal with the problem. Meanwhile, more people become unknowing victims of these synthetic poisons.

AN EXPERIMENT

Effect of Fertilizer on Algae Growth

Use masking tape to label three custard dishes A, B, and C. Put 20 milliliters of tap water in each dish, using a graduated cylinder from science class. Buy some fertilizer pellets that contain 5 parts nitrogen, 10 parts phosphorus, and 5 parts potassium. Place three of these in dish A. Add six pellets to dish B. Do not add any to dish C. That is the control.

Buy some algae in a pet store. Or collect it from a local pond. Put some algae in each dish. Cover each dish with plastic wrap. Put the dishes in a sunny place or under a light. Watch the growth of algae daily until some algae start to die.

In which dish do algae grow fastest? Slowest? In which do they die first? Explain your observations.

CHAPTER 4:
HAZARDOUS SUBSTANCES IN SURFACE WATER

Clean surface water normally contains a variety of living things. No one type of organism prevails. Bacteria levels are low, and oxygen levels are high in clean surface water.

Water can be contaminated with toxic chemicals from waste substances such as sewage, animal manure, soil, and organic debris. All organic substances use up oxygen to some extent, and so if water is overloaded with too much organic waste, the bacteria that decompose the waste use up all the oxygen and life cannot exist in the water.

The same thing occurs when too many nitrates or phosphates get into water. Their presence causes algae to grow so abundantly that bacteria cannot decompose organic waste fast enough. The result is foul-smelling water, loaded with dead organic debris. This process is called *eutrophication.*

A hazardous waste site in New York State.
Photo courtesy New York State Department of Environmental Conservation

There are still other toxic substances in water. These include inorganic chemicals (acids, toxic metals) and synthetic organic chemicals. Inorganic wastes do not support bacteria, while organic wastes do. Toxic organic wastes come from pesticides, detergents, oil, and industrial wastes.

SHOULD WE DRINK THE WATER?

During and after World War II, industrial development made America rich. Although people could afford better and more costly things, they spent little money on sewage treatment. They continued to discard organic waste into large bodies of water.

Then they saw the importance of removing floating solids from sewage water. Large concrete sewage treatment tanks were built to allow time for those solids to settle to the bottom. The water was then pumped into nearby streams or lakes. The solid matter was partly broken down in tanks. It was then placed in landfills or spread on soil as fertilizer.

TESTING A RIVER FOR TOXIC SUBSTANCES

During the 1940s and 1950s, city people noticed that their rivers were getting dirtier. Scientists took samples from different parts of rivers. They collected bottom samples from places all along a river's course. Then they examined these samples to see which organisms were living in the clean sections and which in the dirty sections.

In the table you can see how a river is changed by pollution. In the part where the water is clean, it is high in oxygen. It will often contain a variety of fish, insects, clams, and other animals. All of them need high levels of oxygen. They will be the first to disappear if the oxygen level falls. If the water supports a great variety of species, we know the environment is balanced and the water is clean.

When organic substances, including sewage, from a city or industry enter a river, the bacteria that feed on organic matter increase. The greater number of bacteria use up more oxygen, and the oxygen level decreases. A *zone of decline of oxygen* is created where the waste is discharged. So-called trash fish (carp and catfish) live in this area of low oxygen.

The *damage zone* comes next. Here the oxygen is nearly gone, and only a few animals survive. Hardly any fish are found, and few varieties of life other than sludge worms, sewage-fly larvae, other larvae, and anaerobic bacteria exist. Such bacteria can live only in low-oxygen conditions. A *zone of recovery* follows the damage zone. Here the water is clear, allowing sunlight to enter. Water plants can now grow and make oxygen through photosynthesis. This in turn allows more clean-water life to appear.

The zones in a polluted river.

Zones of Pollution

	Clean Water	Decline	Damage	Recovery
high Oxygen Level low	Origin of Pollution→			
Physical Traits	Clear; no bottom sludge	Floating solids; sludge	Murky; bottom sludge	Floating solids; sludge
Fish Present	Game, pan, a variety	Carp and catfish	None	Carp and catfish
Bottom-dwelling Animals Present	Caddisfly; stonefly; freshwater forms	Bloodworms; snails	Sludge worm; sewage-fly and midge-fly larvae; bloodworms	Bloodworms; snails

If more than one source of sewage or other waste discharge occurs along the stream, the zone of damage may stretch many miles downstream. Such conditions may occur along rivers in cities and industrial areas.

CHLORINE AND DRINKING WATER

The effects of human exposure for a long time to small amounts of toxic organic chemicals have not been fully studied. Yet our folly in waste disposal has created a huge laboratory of rivers, and many of us are the guinea pigs. Evidence of the damage comes from a study of Mississippi River water. The shores of this river are crowded with industries and sewage-treatment plants.

Starting in 1949, according to *Laying Waste* by Michael Brown, an environmental group found forty-eight synthetic organic chemicals in the Mississippi River. Many of the chemicals contained chlorine. Several chemicals were present even in treated drinking water taken from the river. While the contamination increased, so did the cancer rate among New Orleans residents.

A later survey showed that the New Orleans death rate from cancer between 1951 and 1969 was 32 percent greater than the national rate. Anywhere from 73 to 200 synthetic organics, heavy metals, pesticides, and other chemicals have been found in the city's water.

Another example is the Hudson River, where other chlorine-containing compounds (PCBs) invaded the water from 1950 to 1970. Rates of rectal and other digestive cancers increased 65 percent in Poughkeepsie during that time. Was it mere chance that chloroform, trichloroethylene, and carbon tetrachloride (all of which contain chlorine) appeared in the river during that same time? Some of these chlorinated hydrocarbons are released into water supplies by industrial waste discharge.

But there is strong evidence that some chlorinated hydrocarbons are formed another way. Chlorine is used in water-treatment plants to kill bacteria that cause deadly diseases. Drinking water treated with chlorine is used by 75 percent of Americans. The chlorine could combine with organic matter in water to form certain chlorinated hydrocarbons. Those who drink chlorinated water have a 93 percent greater risk of getting rectal cancer, and a 53 percent greater risk of bladder cancer, than those people who do not drink chlorinated water. These statistics come from a study prepared in 1974 by the Environmental Defense Fund in Washington, D.C.

THE CUYAHOGA AND LAKE ERIE: A SUCCESS STORY

The Cuyahoga River runs through the industrial heart of Cleveland, Ohio. For many years, it was a dump site for untreated sewage, oil, steel-making waste, chemical wastes, city runoff, and garbage. Samples taken from the river bottom showed that the hazardous-substance level was so high that even sludge worms could not live there.

The Cuyahoga flows into the western end of Lake Erie, our nation's fourth-largest lake. But the lake was dying. Phosphates were causing increased algal growth. As we saw earlier, increased algal growth cuts off light, causing the algae to die. The increase in the organisms that decompose dead algae consumes oxygen. Without light or oxygen in the lake water, food chains were disrupted. Valuable fish, such as walleye and white bass, decreased.

The aftermath of a fire caused by chemical wastes on the Cuyahoga River in Cleveland, Ohio.

Photo, The Plain Dealer

The trash fish were abundant. Toxic chemicals were found in game fish. Sport fishing vanished. So did the cash it brought to Lake Erie's shore.

Lake Erie, a major resource, was at risk. This lake is the source of 4.4 billion gallons of fresh water used daily by Cleveland. Its loss meant the same amount of water would have to be treated daily by treatment plants.

A public outcry brought billions of federal dollars and the start of cleanup programs around the lake. Water-pollution-control equipment was added to Cleveland's steel mills. The city's water-treatment plant was improved. Some factories were closed because they had been polluting the lake with their industrial wastes. As the water improved, walleye returned in abundance, as did other sport fish.

Despite all this success, some people remain worried about the future of the Cuyahoga River and Lake Erie. Pollution has been reduced, but toxic chemicals and toxic metals stay trapped in bottom muck. They will take decades to decay. City sewage treatment has improved, but sharp cuts in federal funds may stall programs designed to improve water quality.

OIL SPILLS

In March 1978, an oil tanker named the *Amoco Cadiz* spilled 68 million gallons of oil into the sea off the coast of France. The environmental impact was immediate and terrible. Clean, white beaches were coated with oil that felt like hot fudge. Sensitive salt marshes, bays, and oyster beds were coated with it. It was the world's worst oil spill.

The estimated death toll was 20,000 birds, 10,000 fish, and thousands of clams, lobsters, and crabs. Acres of seaweed and marsh grass also died. Shellfish have not yet returned to the spill site.

Such body counts, however, are only part of the story. Gauging the long-term impact on sea life is difficult. And oil spills have a direct economic effect on people, especially fishermen and resort owners.

Scientists who collect samples at the scene of a spill usually don't have a sample taken from the same area prior to the spill. Thus, they have no way to measure the damage. Oil, moreover, changes rapidly in water. It evaporates, mixes, spreads out, becomes thicker in some places and thinner in others. All of this poses constantly changing conditions for scientists.

No two spills are alike. Their effects on ocean life depend on what kind of oil is spilled, where it is spilled, the season, weather conditions, and cleanup methods used.

In March 1989, the worst oil spill in U.S. history occurred in Prince William Sound in southern Alaska. An oil tanker, the *Exxon Valdez*, ran aground on a reef shortly after leaving the port of Valdez with 250,000 barrels of oil. More than ten million gallons of oil spilled into a sensitive environment. Thousands of sea birds, sea otters, sea lions, bald eagles, walruses, and fish were killed. Food chains were disrupted as contaminated animals were eaten by others not yet contaminated.

All of this happened at the worst time of year, when millions of herring were supposed to move into the sound to spawn. The herring, along with millions of salmon and halibut, were killed. Some ate oil-soaked prey. Some took in oil through their gills. The loss to the herring fisheries was $12 million; the salmon fisheries' loss was $120 million.

This accident caused lawmakers to ask tough questions. Should oil exploration in Alaska be slowed, or even stopped? Should larger areas of the state be protected from development? If the United States holds back the pumping of Alaskan oil, how will the country satisfy its hunger for energy?

Until the *Exxon Valdez* hit a reef, such questions did not seem so urgent. But this single disaster made people think that the United States must take a hard look at its dependence on oil and its lack of a sound national energy policy.

Laws and policies were ignored throughout the *Exxon Valdez* disaster. Against state and federal laws, the captain left the ship on autopilot, under the command of an inexperienced third mate who lacked a Coast Guard license. After the accident, more violations occurred. The seven oil companies operating in Alaska had been required to file a plan for dealing with any oil spill. The first thing to do in case of a spill was to boom it—surround it with floating barriers to contain it. The next task was to skim it—suck up floating oil with vacuums mounted on vessels. The third step was to either burn the oil or spread it out with detergents.

Things, however, did not go according to plan. The spill was supposed to be surrounded with booms within three hours. But the only containment barge in Valdez was being repaired. Ten hours passed before the barge could be repaired and brought to the scene.

According to the plan, seven skimmers should have been on the scene within five hours. Instead, three arrived twelve hours later and did not begin work for another eighteen hours. Five days later, the oil slick extended across forty miles of the seventy-mile-long sound. And months later, the slick covered thousands of square miles.

The cleanup would take months, or even years. Experts guessed that it would cost Exxon at least $500 million. Yet that amount was only ten percent of Exxon's $5 billion profits for 1988.

Critics questioned why President Bush did not take charge of the cleanup during the first few days. By then it was clear that neither Exxon nor the Coast Guard could do the job. Two weeks after the accident, President Bush ordered federal help in the cleanup. But he claimed that this was not a matter for the federal government. It was up to Exxon to clean up after itself.

Meanwhile, what about the fishermen whose livelihood was lost? Exxon said that it would pay all claims for losses due to the spill. However, similar promises were given French fishermen after the *Amoco Cadiz* sank, and they have yet to be paid for their losses.

The *Exxon Valdez*'s oil came through the 800-mile Alaska pipeline connecting Valdez to an oil field in

Prudhoe Bay on the northern coast. Concerns about damage to fish and other ocean-dwelling animals had delayed the building of the Alaska pipeline for years. Environmentalists had said it should be built overland through Canada; this would avoid shipping large amounts of oil from Valdez, with its icebergs, reefs, and storms. But the oil industry had claimed that modern technology for tanker navigation and oil-spill cleanup had made such worries obsolete.

The pipeline began operations in 1977 under tight control. But such control became lax in the absence of accidents. Tankers at first could only transport the oil during daylight hours. Later, tanker traffic at night was allowed. The area where captains themselves were required to guide ships was reduced. The full-time, highly trained emergency cleanup crew was replaced with part-time, inexperienced people. The result: since 1977 about forty spills and leaks have occurred in Prince William Sound.

Three months after the Alaskan oil spill, U.S. oil companies announced a new plan to prevent another environmental disaster. The companies will create a network of cleanup crews to handle spills anywhere along U.S. coastlines. Equipment such as oil skimmer boats and chemicals to dissolve the oil will be stored in nineteen areas across the country.

The plan also calls for a five-year program to research oil spills and cleanups. The program will cost between $30 million and $35 million, yet this is a small price to pay compared to the $500 million Exxon spent to clean up Prince William Sound.

Meanwhile, the decade-long debate over drilling for oil in the Arctic National Wildlife Refuge has had the same arguments as the pipeline battle. The oil industry and the Department of the Interior say that this new source of oil is vital to the nation's energy future. They claim it can be pumped out without harm to the environment.

Environmentalists predict damage to wildlife, mainly through oil spills. The area is a haven for caribou, birds, and many other animals. Even in Alaska, which gets 85 percent of its income from oil taxes, support for the oil industry declined after the *Exxon Valdez* spill. At best, drilling for oil in the refuge might provide enough oil for ten years. Another wilderness would be destroyed. And then the country would again be faced with what to do next.

Finding more oil is not the answer to our energy needs. We need instead a sound national policy for energy conservation. The pressure to drill more oil wells in Alaska stems mainly from our rate of energy use. During the Reagan presidency, auto speed limits rose, stricter fuel-efficiency standards for new cars were postponed, and research into other energy sources was cut. The result: the U.S. appetite for oil has risen a lot.

We should get tough about conservation. An increase in the federal gasoline tax would discourage unnecessary driving. Part of the tax money could be used to develop nonfossil energy sources. We could also require the auto industry to build cars that use less fuel. That could save twice the amount of oil each day that was spilled in Prince William Sound.

Conservation will not be easy. But the public's horror

over fouled beaches and dying animals could be a good thing. It could cause people to save energy. If that happens, the wreck of the *Exxon Valdez* will not be a total disaster.

It would be impractical and unfair to halt Alaska's oil business completely. But exploration for oil and its production can be limited. Better environmental safeguards can be put in place.

In the end, the battle for Alaska's future may be decided by the other forty-nine states. If Americans can abandon wasteful habits, Alaska will be under less pressure to squander its precious wilderness.

Despite the immediate massive impact of oil spills like those of the *Amoco Cadiz* and the *Exxon Valdez*, scientists consider other leaks to be more dangerous. The slow, constant dripping of oil from sewer pipelines, harbor spills, and storage tank leaks are more damaging to the environment. Why? Because the affected areas never have time to recover from one dose of oil before the next one comes along.

NEW YORK CITY WATERS

Most solid wastes left over after sewage treatment are burned, buried, or used as fertilizer. Such wastes, called *sludge,* are also dumped in the ocean from some coastal cities in New York and New Jersey.

New York City went to court to fight the federal Ocean Dumping Prohibition Act of 1977. This act set a deadline of 1982 to stop the dumping of sewage sludge. But the dumping continued twelve miles off the New Jersey shore. Each year, some 20 million tons of contaminated sludge, dredge spoils, and industrial acid wastes were dumped there, within fifteen miles of land. In 1986, the dump site was moved to 106 miles offshore.

How was New York City able to successfully challenge the 1977 act? The city brought evidence that the ocean could absorb sewage sludge better, at lower cost, and with less health risk to humans than burning or dumping in landfills.

Meanwhile, the EPA permits New York City to construct more buildings and factories. These produce more waste. Much of it is piped directly into the Hudson River (150 million gallons a day) and East River (50 to 100 million gallons a day). In 1984, Congress passed the Water Quality Renewal Act. This law gave New York City until 1987 to clean up the Hudson and East rivers. The city is building new water-treatment plants under court order, but they will not be ready to operate for ten to twenty years.

Thus, the 1987 act was not enforced by the EPA. How do we know? Because the Hudson and East rivers have not yet been cleaned up.

In 1988, Congress passed a modified version of the Ocean Dumping Prohibition Act. It set a deadline of December 31, 1991, for ending ocean dumping of industrial waste and city sludge. It also created a trust fund financed by the fees and penalties paid by sludge dumpers if they keep on dumping after the deadline.

Yet some experts believe that waste should be dumped in the deep ocean. Few fish are caught there, and the deep ocean has the greatest ability to handle human wastes of any habitat on the planet.

The coastal ocean, however, is fragile and unprotected. Waste that is burned or dumped on land flows downhill and eventually ends up there. Many people believe the revised act makes this problem worse. They feel we can protect the coastal ocean only by dumping our waste in the deep ocean, at depths of 3,000 feet or more.

In the next chapter, we will look at more laws designed to clean up our water.

ACTIVITIES

1. A Local River

Report on a river in your area. Name its source. Draw a diagram of its course. Include any towns it passes through.

List any industries that add materials to this river. What, if anything, will be taken away from the water as it flows through your community? List and explain.

2. Senses and Streams

Take a trip to a spot upstream on a nearby river. Describe the river at that point. Tell how it smells, looks, sounds, and feels. List any materials you find in the water that do not belong in or along the river (tires, cans, and so forth).

Take a trip downstream, just beyond the town. Describe the river as you did above.

Compare your findings. What are your conclusions?

3. Your Water-Treatment System

Look into your community's water-treatment system. Report back to your class with answers to the following questions: Does your area have a water-treatment plant? If not, why not? If there is a plant, what process does the waste go through? Where is it taken after it is treated? Where is the plant located? What are the advantages and disadvantages of this location?

CHAPTER 5:
CONTROLLING WATER POLLUTION

We can fight surface water pollution in a variety of ways. One technique is to prevent pollution before it starts by passing laws against it. To this end, Congress has been setting water-quality standards since the late 1960s.

FEDERAL WATER POLLUTION CONTROL ACT OF 1972

In 1972, Congress passed the Water Pollution Control Act. This act required the EPA to set up national standards for the control of water pollutants. All cities and towns had to install water-treatment facilities by 1977. All industries had to use the best practical technology for treating wastes by 1977, and by 1983 the best available technology.

One aim of this act was to make all American waters safe for fishing and swimming by mid-1983. Another goal was to stop the release of all chemicals (zero discharge) into our waters by 1985. The act allowed factories to dump chemicals into American rivers only if they had a permit approved by the EPA. The act also appropriated $24.6 billion to be used for cleaning up the nation's waters between 1972 and 1977. Another $18 billion was given to the states for the building of water-treatment plants.

Between 1972 and 1982, many water-treatment plants were built. The federal government has given $45 billion in construction money; state contributions have raised total spending above $60 billion. Some 4,500 new plants are operating and about 8,200 more are being built.

Since its passage, the 1972 Federal Water Pollution Control Act has been attacked by industries, some scientists, and environmental groups, according to an article by Oliver Houck in *National Geographic.* The goal of zero discharge was said to be unrealistic. The act did not recognize that some wastes are toxic and others are not. It also did not take into account that some wastes are *biodegradable.* This means they will decompose and become harmless after a while. The 1972 act was also said to be too costly in comparison with the limited benefits it would provide.

CLEAN WATER ACT OF 1977

After much pressure, Congress replaced the 1972 act with the Clean Water Act of 1977. This act also established a goal of zero discharge by 1985 but applied it chiefly to toxic chemicals.

It postponed the deadline for industrial use of the best available technology to 1984. (This deadline was not met.) The act also allowed the EPA to grant exemptions to industries where costs would outweigh benefits. For some pesticides and heavy metals, the deadline was postponed to mid-1987, and again, the EPA could grant exemptions. For toxic chemicals, the best-technology deadline was 1984 (this deadline, too, was not met).

THE EPA AND THE CLEAN WATER ACT

Although Congress had passed the Clean Water Act in 1977, the administration in 1978 began to weaken its effect. First, the EPA proposed changes in the clean-water rules. These changes would permit states to lower their water-quality standards.

Second, other changes would delay pollution controls on toxic discharges by industry. Such delays would last several years beyond the time companies needed to install controls.

Third, EPA's funds were reduced each year from 1978 on. These funds were needed to enforce environmental laws, including this act.

One of the biggest changes in the clean-water program was a partial retreat to the low water-quality standards of the late 1960s. Cities on the West Coast and in Alaska had long dumped their sewage into deep, fast-moving ocean waters. These cities claimed they should not be required to build costly water-treatment plants.

Congress agreed. It passed the modified 1977 Clean Water Act, excusing these cities from EPA requirements. Those cities, however, were required to prove they were not polluting the ocean.

But by the time all this occurred, the EPA had bowed to similar pressures by other coastal cities. Some scientists argue that deep ocean dump sites near active currents— not shallow sites like those used by New York and Boston—may be the safest and cheapest places to dispose of such wastes.

Industries have spent more than $30 billion in their efforts to comply with the standards set by the Clean Water Act. They have managed to clean up some pollutants, but they have not eliminated toxic organic chemicals. Even the Cuyahoga River is polluted with toxic industrial solvents, because heavy metals and low levels of toxics enter it along with water running off city streets.

But the poor record is not entirely industry's fault. During the Reagan administration, the EPA did not set health standards for most toxics. And the agency has been slow to release standards for municipal water-treatment plants.

Since 1972, the federal government's efforts to control water pollution have focused on effluent from industry and municipal sewage-treatment plants. The Clean Water Act was changed again in 1987. It now authorizes another $18 billion between 1987 and 1996 for more water-treatment plants. The 1987 act also extends the EPA's deadline for requiring cities to control storm-water runoff. Nevertheless, in 1989 the Sierra Club and other environmental groups went to court to press for a tightening of the pollution permits for New York City's fourteen water-treatment plants. The Sierra Club said the plants could not handle the waste that had resulted from greater numbers of people. The plants were often taking in more waste water than they could treat, and this meant that raw, untreated waste was being dumped into the rivers around the city.

The environmental organizations also wanted better laws to prohibit the dumping of heavy metals and other toxic chemicals into the sewage treatment system. They said that at least 4,000 pounds of toxic metals were entering the sewers each day, making the sewage treatment plants work less effectively. The toxic metals ended up in the sludge that was later dumped into the Atlantic at the site 106 miles offshore. Each year, New York City's sludge adds more than 1.6 million pounds of toxic metals to the ocean, according to the Oceanic Society.

PRETREATMENT OF TOXIC SUBSTANCES

More than half the nation's 60,000 factories discharge wastes into sewage systems. These companies are required by the Clean Water Act to pretreat such wastes to remove toxics before the waste reaches sewage plants, which are designed chiefly to process household sewage. Sludge without toxic wastes can be recycled into fertilizer. Industrial sewage sludge loaded with toxics, however, must be disposed of like any other hazardous material—buried in landfills, burned, or dumped into the ocean. All three methods harm the environment. Large amounts of such toxic wastes are costly to dispose of.

Toxic substances can interfere with the workings of a water-treatment plant. The toxics can kill bacteria used to digest the sewage in the secondary waste water treatment. This destroys the treatment process. Moreover, the toxics pass through the plant untreated.

The only way to prevent toxics from damaging sewage-treatment plants is to separate the toxic waste from other waste before it reaches the plant. But the government's pretreatment program is under attack. Some towns and industries say that certain communities should be exempt from the government's pretreatment program. They would provide their own pretreatment programs and set their own standards.

Conservationists are against this idea. They say it would allow too many toxics into our waters. It is true that many communities already have sewage-treatment plants. But, as we have seen, these plants can do little to prevent toxics from passing through them.

But industry officials fear the government will force them to remove wastes that are adequately removed by sewage plants. They question the need to build separate treatment plants.

CLEANING WATER WITH WATER HYACINTHS

Water-treatment facilities use different methods to try to remove disease-causing bacteria, toxic chemicals, and other pollutants. But water treatment is costly. And, in large cities with huge water needs, the treatment plants may have difficulty keeping up with demands for clean water.

A few cities have tried something different. They use the water hyacinth to clean their water. This plant can double its size in two weeks. Ten plants can multiply to 600,000 in less than a year.

How do water hyacinths clean water? As they float, their roots dangle in the water. Chemicals that pollute water, such as nitrates and phosphates, are taken up by the roots. Water hyacinths also absorb pesticides, toxic wastes, and even some heavy metals.

Water hyacinths take twenty times longer to clean polluted water than a water-treatment facility, and they can only be used where the weather is warm all year. But they don't need special materials or outside energy sources or much care. So these plants can clean water at half the cost of other water-treatment methods.

A number of towns in the United States and Canada have taken the water hyacinth method a step further. They have built artificial marshes that clean waste water better than sewage-treatment plants. These marshes also provide a wildlife habitat.

But the biggest advantage of this system is its lower cost. The construction cost is about one-half that of sewage-treatment plants, and wetlands maintain themselves because they purify waste water through natural biological decay.

Such a system would work well in many rural parts of the United States and Canada. According to a report by the Conservation Foundation, more than 100 million Americans are served by water-treatment plants that do not meet standards set by the Clean Water Act. The EPA estimates that $80 billion would be needed to build new plants or improve the old ones. Many of these old plants are in small towns that cannot afford the millions of dollars needed to meet the standards. For such small towns, the artificial wetland idea could and does work.

WHO WILL CLEAN UP YELLOW CREEK?

Yellow Creek flows through Middlesboro, Kentucky, a coal-mining town in the Appalachian Mountains. For many years, the creek has been polluted with a black substance from the town sewage plant. This waste enters the sewage plant from a tannery that makes shoe leather from rawhide. Sometimes the discharge from the plant killed fish, but the damage did not appear permanent.

In 1965, however, the tannery started a special process that uses 250 chemicals. Certain pollutants, including chromium and lead, poured into Yellow Creek. Water from the creek is used by the townspeople for drinking. Birth defects and cancer increased in the area, according to editorials appearing in the *Middlesboro Press*, the local

The polluted Yellow Creek in Middlesboro, Kentucky.
Photo, Courier Journal *and* Louisville Times

newspaper. A citizens' group has been battling to get the tannery to clean up or get out.

The people of Middlesboro have found out for certain what residents in other towns only suspect: their sewage plant does not work. The creek is dark red and black where the sewage plant empties into it. It is gray-green downstream. The colors found in Yellow Creek may be partly due to coal-mine drainage that contains black iron pyrite, rust-colored iron hydroxide, and two types of iron sulfate—one green and the other yellow-orange.

Local people now face increases in their sewer bills because the town would not ask the company to clean up. Complicating matters is a 1970 contract that made the city legally responsible for disposing of the tannery's sewage. The Clean Water Act left it up to local governments to decide how thoroughly a factory had to clean its waste water before sending it on to the town's sewage plant.

Critics of this part of the act say that cities often bow easily to pressure from local industry to ease up on enforcement of pretreatment standards.

The experts, of course, disagree on the cause and extent of the problems at Yellow Creek. Nearby Vanderbilt University measured silt from the creek bed against water-quality standards. It found 3,000 times the safe amount of cadmium; 4,000 times the safe limit of chromium; and 1,500 times the safe level of lead. These toxic metals cause severe headaches, kidney damage, heart disease, and birth defects. An EPA study, however, turned up no dangerous levels of toxic materials in the

Hazardous waste from the tannery flowing into the
sewage-treatment plant in Middlesboro, Kentucky.
Photo, Courier Journal *and* Louisville Times

creek's water or silt. There are possible explanations for the contradictory outcome of the Vanderbilt study and the EPA study. Cadmium, chromium, and lead may originate from the coal in the nearby coal mine. Also, the EPA samples were taken from different sites than those taken by Vanderbilt University.

AN EXPERIMENT

Effects of Phosphate Detergents on Fish Breathing Rates

Let's simulate the effects of a common toxic substance on stream fish. This experiment will not harm the fish if done properly, and it should be done only with the help of a teacher. You will need several medium-sized goldfish from a pet store. You will also need three 600-milliliter glass jars. Get some distilled water in a supermarket. Label the jars A, B, and C.

Choose two powdered detergents. One can be for laundry, and the other for dishwashing. Or both can be for laundry use. But be sure that only one of them has phosphates. Read the ingredients on the package.

Remember, you are not trying to kill the fish or make them suffer. Goldfish, of course, do not occur naturally in streams. But carp do, and carp are cousins of goldfish. Both carp and goldfish can stand certain amounts of toxic materials. This is why you are using goldfish. Try to use goldfish that are all the same size.

Place a fish in 500 milliliters of distilled water. Do not use tap water. You do not know which chemical contaminants may be in it. Distilled water has no minerals or contaminants in it.

Watch how the fish opens and closes its gill covers. Each time it does this, count it as one breath. Time the breathing rate for one minute. Do this five times. Then calculate the average breathing rate per minute. Leave the fish in that jar for now.

Pour 500 milliliters of distilled water into each of the remaining two jars. Measure ½ teaspoon of the no-phosphate detergent. Place it in one jar. Measure a level teaspoon of the same detergent. Place it in the other jar. Stir both jars well.

Now take the fish whose breathing rate you observed and put it in the ½-teaspoon jar. First watch for signs of stress. If the fish floats or seems unable to control its balance, transfer it back to the distilled water jar immediately. Then discard the contents of the ½-teaspoon jar, and prepare a new solution at a lower dose.

If, however, the fish looks and acts well in the ½-teaspoon jar, time its breathing rate per minute five more times. Figure out the average breathing rate per minute.

Now transfer the fish back to the first jar for two minutes. This will wash off any traces of detergent from its gills.

Then transfer it to the jar with the full teaspoon of detergent. Watch for signs of stress. If all looks well, time the breathing rate per minute for another five minutes. Get the average. Transfer the animal back to the first jar for washing.

Rinse the jars and then repeat all the above with the phosphate detergent. Use the same amounts and measurements. But be extra careful. Watch for signs of a buildup of film or foam around the fish's gills. If this occurs, remove the fish and adjust the dose. Record all your observations in your notebook.

With which detergent did the fish show more stress? The greater average breathing rate? How would fish taken from a river or lake react to this experiment? To find out, use an aquarium net or dip net to collect several minnows or other species. See what happens.

CHAPTER 6:
GROUNDWATER CONTAMINATION

About half of all Americans depend on groundwater, much of it untreated, for drinking. Several major cities such as Miami, Florida, and Memphis, Tennessee, depend entirely on groundwater. All 2.5 million people in Nassau and Suffolk counties, Long Island, New York, also depend on it. Ninety-five percent of all rural Americans get their water from underground wells. More than a third of the people in over thirty states drink public water that is groundwater.

Groundwater use is increasing 25 percent each decade. Why? Because it is needed for farming. Most of the people in the grain-producing states of Nebraska, Iowa, and South Dakota depend on it.

SYNTHETIC ORGANICS

Only 2 percent of America's groundwater in public and private wells is now known to be polluted. But synthetic organic chemicals are special threats to it. Because of the lack of oxygen underground, not enough bacteria exist there to break down the synthetics. What's more, many toxic chemicals do not have the attraction for soil that allows the soil to absorb them as they seep downward. Chlorinated hydrocarbons are especially difficult to get rid of. Recall that they persist for a long time and can biomagnify. They are also not soluble in water. Also recall that aquifers flow slowly. Thus, once contaminated, they may remain so for thousands of years.

So it is not surprising that these chemicals are found in hundreds of wells nationwide. Before state officials closed them, several wells in Pennsylvania, New York, and New Jersey had more than 1,000 ppb of trichloroethylene (TCE). Many experts believe that the poisoning of our groundwater is the greatest environmental threat to public health.

But the federal government apparently does not agree. The 1972 Water Pollution Control Act recognized a federal interest in safeguarding both surface water and groundwater. The EPA reports serious groundwater contamination in at least forty states, yet the EPA still has no effective national system to monitor groundwater and protect it from chemical contamination. Nearly every state east of the Mississippi River has groundwater problems, as do the nonindustrial, lightly populated western states. Some drinking water wells are closed in twenty-five states. The states may be willing to do something about the pollution, but they seldom have enough money.

Burnt Fly Bog, a landfill in New Jersey.

Photo, New Jersey Newsphotos

Drinking water wells are closed in these states:

California	Missouri
Colorado	New Hampshire
Connecticut	New Jersey
Delaware	New Mexico
Florida	New York
Illinois	North Carolina
Iowa	Ohio
Louisiana	Pennsylvania
Maine	Rhode Island
Maryland	Tennessee
Massachusetts	Texas
Michigan	Wisconsin
Minnesota	

Thirty-three synthetic organic chemicals are often found in groundwater. Of these, the most common are chlorinated solvents like TCE, PCE, chloroform, and carbon tetrachloride. The levels of these chemicals are much higher in groundwater than in surface water.

HOW AQUIFERS WORK

Underground water movements can be complex. Water reaches an aquifer through one or several *recharge zones*, places where surface water seeps underground. Streams, lakes, marshes, and swamps are essential recharge areas.

Water quality in an aquifer depends on the region's geologic conditions. For example, a city or industrial landfill located on a thick layer of natural clay may pose little threat to an aquifer below, since water cannot

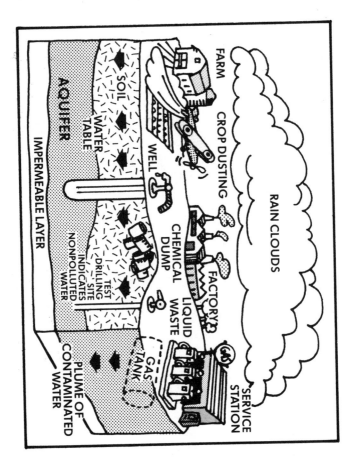

Groundwater becomes contaminated by buried or discarded toxics that reach the aquifer.

usually seep through clay. But one located on sandy soil, or even sandstone, is a big threat. Because much of the West is sandstone, nonindustrial states there are having contamination problems. Much of their groundwater flows from and is contaminated by nearby states with industrial landfills.

As rain falls on a landfill, it seeps, or *leaches*, through the buried waste products. It forms a fluid, called *leachate*. This fluid gradually drains out of the dump and into groundwater. Five dangerous industrial organic chemicals are often found in this leachate: vinyl chloride, TCE, PCE, trichloroethane (TCA), and dichloropropane (DCP). They may cause liver and kidney damage, cancer, and genetic damage in laboratory animals, as explained in Theodore Goldfarb's *Taking Sides*.

PROBLEMS AND PROGRESS IN MEASURING CONTAMINATION

Chemicals leach down from a site and then spread out underground. Pollutants come from many sources and move in different directions within the aquifer. So it is hard to be sure if old wells or the 500,000 new ones dug each year are safe. The groundwater may be heavily toxic in one place, but safe only several hundred feet away. Also, polluted groundwater may take years to travel underground to another water supply.

Monitoring different sites is expensive. To do this, test wells must be drilled at many spots along an aquifer. Each test well costs many thousands of dollars. Since the federal government does not require industries to do their own tests, the task is up to individual states. But they cannot do it because they don't have enough money.

Unfortunately, neither the EPA nor state agencies have any control over the basic cause of groundwater contamination—bad land-use practices. Stricter land-use controls at the recharge areas of an aquifer would solve the problem. Government policies should consider the close link between homes, roads, industry, and waste disposal in order to preserve groundwater quality.

What land-use methods are effective for this purpose? Low-population-density zoning laws, under which taxable property would be zoned to preserve open space rather than be crowded with homes, roads, and industries, are an answer.

This low-density use would relieve some groundwater problems, but land zoning is done by city officials. Some of these people dislike seeing taxable land zoned to keep out development. Their version of progress is to build more homes, roads, and industries. This kind of land use, which threatens water supplies, brings in more jobs and produces more tax money.

LANDFILLS, PITS, AND LAGOONS

Landfills are a great threat to groundwater. Most of the 92 billion pounds of hazardous wastes produced each year are dumped in landfills. Only 20 percent of these wastes are dumped properly.

Lipari Toxic Waste Landfill in Pitman, New Jersey, considered to be the worst landfill in New Jersey and the fifth worst in the nation, according to the EPA.

Photo, New Jersey Newsphotos

Pits and lagoons are used for storage, treatment, and disposal of industrial, city, farming, mining, and oil-brine liquid wastes. There were nearly 250,000 toxic pits, lagoons, and landfills in the United States at last count. According to the EPA, 90 percent of pits and lagoons are not monitored—that is, few wells have been dug to measure the effects pit leachates have on groundwater quality. The EPA also found 98 percent of these dump sites within a mile of underground drinking water; 93 percent threatened groundwater supplies, according to a League of Women Voters report.

Some of the toxic waste chemicals at the sites leak from rotting storage drums. Some glisten in thick, black lagoons. And some are placed underground in fiberglass tanks in a vain attempt to prevent leakage. Many hazardous waste disposal areas are created by illegal dumping. They are, of course, an even greater threat because they sometimes remain unknown to authorities for years.

UNDERGROUND GASOLINE STORAGE TANKS

Hundreds of thousands of underground storage tanks filled with gasoline exist in the United States. Most of these tanks were built in the 1950s and 1960s when the gasoline industry was growing. Made of steel designed to last twenty years, the tanks eventually corrode. About

Leaking drums at a dump in New York State.
Photo courtesy New York State Department
of Environmental Conservation

100,000 leaks have been reported already. Half the leaky tanks are located underground in sandy soil.

Once gasoline has leached into groundwater, it is nearly impossible to remove. One gallon of gasoline can contaminate the water supply of 50,000 people at the parts-per-billion level. Thus, gasoline contamination of an aquifer may make the water unusable for decades.

IS OUR GOVERNMENT PROTECTING US?

The Safe Drinking Water Act of 1974 allowed the EPA to establish national standards for drinking water contaminants. In 1975, the EPA adopted temporary standards. Included were standards for ten inorganic chemicals, radioactivity, cloudiness, bacteria, four pesticides, and two herbicides.

This 1974 act does not require local governments or water companies to test their water for other pollutants, nor does it provide protection for the 60 million people in rural America. But it does require the EPA to change its rules so as to keep up with the latest information on health effects.

These temporary standards have not yet been changed, however. The EPA has proposed no standards for synthetic organics found in groundwater, much of which is used as drinking water. But some states have begun setting temporary standards for a few of these materials. The standards allow those states to close wells if specific levels of the chemicals are found.

Our nation needs legal standards for many toxic organics now found in drinking water, both in rural and urban areas. Second, a groundwater protection framework should be established. In 1980, the EPA proposed such a framework. It included ways to coordinate groundwater protection between state and federal governments. But the plan was never put into effect. The states alone cannot financially support the research needed to protect groundwater. Our country needs a strong partnership between the states and the federal government in this matter.

What about EPA rule-making delays? After all, the Safe Drinking Water Act was passed in 1974. But the agency was not required to enforce its national standards until 1977. As we have seen, the EPA still does not enforce its own laws very well. According to *Hazardous Waste in America* by Epstein, Brown, and Pope, some people in the EPA claim that the large size of the agency prevents it from acting promptly to enforce national drinking water standards.

The Safe Drinking Water Act was modified in 1986. This time, the EPA set national drinking water standards for twenty-six water pollutants. The 1986 act required the EPA to set standards for eighty-three more pollutants by 1989 and for another twenty-five by 1991. However, health officials criticized the EPA for not setting standards for more of the 700 potential pollutants found in drinking water.

IS INDUSTRY PROTECTING US?

Environmental groups do not think that the only reason for the EPA's delays is the agency's large size. They say industry is able, through the courts, to force the EPA to weaken its own standards and thereby allow industry to pollute drinking water. The EPA states that it does not make the laws; it only tries to enforce them.

To what degree, then, should industry protect us from its chemicals? Should it take on the costs and risks of new technologies designed to clean up its industrial wastes? Such costs might lower industry's productivity, because more time might be spent on pollution-control devices and less time on production of goods.

The huge volumes of hazardous industrial waste today are increasing rapidly. Industry normally avoids paying for something that returns no short-term benefit. Without legal obligation, companies are unlikely to use safer disposal methods that will be more costly for them. Lack of strong enforcement of current laws protects industry if victims of hazardous substances sue companies for damages. In short, it pays for industry to keep on dumping the cheap way—into the ground. (In Chapter 10 there is a more complete discussion of disposal techniques.)

New industrial chemicals, meanwhile, keep appearing on the market. They show up at a rate of twenty a week, one thousand a year.

Who, then, is protecting us from groundwater contamination? At present, the answer for many of us is—no one.

EXPERIMENTS

1. Hazardous Organic Wastes in Soil

CAUTION: Do not have any fire or flame nearby when you do this experiment. Be sure the room is well ventilated, and do not taste any of the materials.

Set up three glass jars filled with equal amounts of sand. Label the jars A, B, and C. Pour 10 milliliters of gasoline into one. Using a stop watch, record how long it takes the gasoline to reach the bottom.

Pour the same amount of cleaning fluid or liquid fabric softener into the second jar. Record as before.

Then pour 10 milliliters of nail polish remover into the third jar. Time its movements as before. This substance contains acetone, a carcinogen.

Which of these three organic materials reached the bottom of the sand most quickly? Which moved quickest sideways?

Conduct this experiment again. But this time, mix 5 milliliters of each substance with 5 milliliters of water before pouring it over the sand. What differences, if any, do you notice?

Perform both parts of this experiment again, using gravel instead of sand. Are there any differences?

2. Pollution by Organic Matter

Bacteria help break down organic matter in both soil and water. Many bacteria are present when the amount of organic matter in a water supply is high. Thus, you can measure the organic matter in water by measuring the size of the bacteria population.

You will need three different water samples. Take them from such sources as dishwater, well water, tap water, or water from a mud puddle or swamp. Also get three test tubes, a test-tube rack, masking tape, a 50-milliliter graduated cylinder, an eyedropper, a grease pencil, and methylene blue dye from your science teacher.

First, make a methylene blue solution. Add 2 drops of dye to 20 milliliters of water. Bacteria act on the dye. They cause it to lose color. The more bacteria in a water sample, the faster the color is broken down.

Mark three test tubes A, B, and C with a grease pencil. Put five milliliters of a different water sample in each tube. Record in your notebook the kind of water you put in each tube.

Add 20 drops of the dye solution to each sample. Put the tubes in a test-tube rack. Watch them every ten minutes for an hour.

In which tubes does the color disappear first? Which water sample has the largest number of bacteria? Which sample has the greatest amount of organic matter? The least?

Record all your observations in your notebook.

CHAPTER 7:
PESTICIDES AS HAZARDOUS SUBSTANCES

Pesticides are chemicals designed to kill pests that prey on food crops, lawns, and gardens. Those pesticides used against insects are called *insecticides.*

Pesticides can cause problems, sometimes even after they have been banned. The pesticide DDT was banned from use in the United States in 1972 after being used since the 1940s. Yet an EPA study showed DDT is still found in many water samples even today, at levels of several hundred parts per trillion. Americans have an average of 5 to 10 ppm of DDT in their body fat, according to Allen Boraiko in an article in *National Geographic.*

Over sixty thousand pesticide formulations are registered with the EPA. These contain some 3,500 chemical compounds. Yet the EPA requires that drinking water be tested for only six of these compounds. Sixty compounds that are not on the EPA list have shown up in the groundwater of thirty states.

Chemicals that are not required to be tested for by the EPA have shown up in the groundwater of thirty states.

Arizona	Missouri
California	Nebraska
Colorado	New Jersey
Connecticut	New York
Florida	North Carolina
Georgia	North Dakota
Hawaii	Ohio
Illinois	Rhode Island
Indiana	South Carolina
Iowa	South Dakota
Kansas	Tennessee
Kentucky	Texas
Maine	Virginia
Maryland	West Virginia
Massachusetts	Wisconsin

We know almost nothing about the effect on humans of the chemicals in pesticides. Perhaps 90 percent of them have not been adequately tested to see if they cause cancer, birth defects, or mutations.

Under a new EPA proposal, states may get federal aid for setting up protection zones for underground wells. States would have to classify aquifers in three categories. Some would be given high priority protection for all uses. Others would be considered sources of drinking water only. Still others would need little protection because they contain water that is unlikely ever to be drunk.

This idea has been opposed by environmentalists

because a large number of groundwater supplies would never be protected.

PESTICIDES IN THE SAN JOAQUIN VALLEY

California's 7,000-square-mile San Joaquin Valley has a serious groundwater-contamination problem. One million people living in the valley have been exposed to a pesticide in their drinking water. It can cause sterility and cancer, according to Boraiko.

The chemical in the pesticide is dibromochloropropane (DBCP), made by Dow Chemical and Shell Chemical. These companies knew there was a link between DBCP and sterility when they started making the pesticide in 1961. DBCP was created to sterilize certain root parasites on farm crops. Tiny amounts of it also sterilized lab animals. Laws at the time required no studies of the effects of DBCP on humans. So Dow and Shell closely watched workers handling DBCP, and suggested exposure limits. But they never tested their workers for sterility. Dow and Shell got government approval to market the chemical. In 1964, Occidental Petroleum also began making DBCP.

New information emerged in 1974. The National Cancer Institute found that DBCP causes cancer in test animals. Although these results were published, no action was taken by the companies, the state, or the EPA. Thus, 6 million more pounds of DBCP were spread across California farms.

Workers harvesting celery in the San Joaquin Valley in California.

Photo courtesy California Farm Bureau Federation

In 1977, Occidental Petroleum found that some of the workers in its factory in Lathrop, California, were sterile. Some Dow and Shell workers in California became sterile as well. The state immediately banned the use of DBCP. The EPA reduced its use on certain crops, but waited two years to ban it.

But the state overlooked the question of whether pesticides could filter down to groundwater. Occidental already knew it was contaminating nearby wells. For years, the company had put DBCP and other wastes into pits and lagoons on its property. In 1978, Occidental finally told the state about its dumping.

Occidental claimed it had observed California reporting requirements. The company also claimed DBCP was tested completely when it was first discovered. It denied that the chemical was a present danger to humans.

Nevertheless, the state and federal governments sued the company in 1979. They claimed it had contaminated groundwater at Lathrop. Occidental agreed to settle out of court. It agreed to pay the cost of cleaning the groundwater.

All of this led to the discovery that pesticides could move down through soil into the aquifers. But this knowledge came too late. For twenty years, California farmers had spread over 3 billion pounds of DBCP over the soil.

After DBCP was banned, the problem did not end. Farmers turned to other pesticides. These, too, are now in California's drinking water. Animal tests show they are highly toxic. They include dichloropropane (DCP), known to cause liver and kidney damage. Another ingredient is ethylene dibromide (EDB), which may cause sterility, cancer, and genetic damage. Water from 1,500 wells in the valley cannot be used for drinking, bathing, or cooking because of this contamination.

THE CASE FOR PESTICIDE USE

During World War II, DDT was sprayed directly on the bodies of soldiers and civilians to control body lice, which spread typhus. DDT was also used to control the spread of malaria, bubonic plague, and sleeping sickness. Thanks mainly to DDT and other chlorinated hydrocarbon insecticides, the lives of at least seven million people have been saved since 1947.

But by 1985, the World Health Organization said that fifty-one of the sixty malaria-bearing mosquito species had become resistant to DDT and the other chlorinated insecticides. As a result, malaria has increased forty times since 1970 in countries where it had nearly been destroyed. To ban insecticides would therefore lead to increased disease and death.

Furthermore, the annual $3 billion that the United States spends on pesticides helps produce $12 billion in crop harvests. Pesticides control pests quickly. They have a long shelf life. They are easily shipped and applied to crops. And they are safe when handled properly. When pests build up resistance to one pesticide, people can switch to others.

The tomato harvest in the San Joaquin Valley.

Photo courtesy California Farm Bureau Federation

THE CASE AGAINST PESTICIDE USE

How do most pests develop resistance to chemicals? When an area is sprayed, most pests are killed. But several survive because they have genes that make them resistant. Most pest species have short life spans. So the few that survive the spraying can reproduce a large number of resistant young in a short time, and each generation of pests has a greater percentage of resistant individuals.

About twenty pest species have become resistant to every pesticide thrown at them. By 1995, more than 1,500 insect pest species could be resistant to insecticides. By the year 2000, all insect pests will probably be resistant.

Humans are often exposed to high levels of pesticides during the production and spraying processes, which can cause serious illness and even death. According to the World Resources Institute, the true number of pesticide-related illnesses each year is in the millions, including 300,000 in the United States.

Injuries and deaths can also occur from pesticide production. In 1975, Virginia officials found that 70 of the 150 employees in a pesticide factory in Hopewell (near Richmond) had been poisoned by kepone—a persistent chlorinated hydrocarbon used as an ant and roach poison. Inside the plant, kepone dust filled the air. It was even in the lunch area. Workers brought it home on their clothes. Twenty-nine of them had uncontrolled shaking, slurred speech, brain and liver damage, and sterility.

also praised by the National Academy of Sciences, which says our food supply could be made safer by applying a uniform standard of little risk rather than none. But environmentalists say that the new policy does not do enough to protect public health. The Natural Resources Defense Council says that the trace-risk standard could be ignored on raw foods. This could be done if the EPA judges that the benefits of a pesticide to the food supply outweigh its risks. And, while a trace amount of a chemical on food might be safe for adults, it might be very risky for children who take in higher levels of pesticides compared to their body weight.

In 1978, Congress set specific standards under FIFRA for testing old and new pesticides. The 1972 FIFRA had required the EPA to study all the active ingredients of pesticides by 1975, but this had not been done by 1978.

Testing was slow because the EPA had not been given enough money or people to do the job. By 1989, the EPA had finished studying only six ingredients in pesticides. The EPA has banned only twelve pesticides from use in the United States. At the current pace, the testing process could go into the next century.

A case in point is alar. This pesticide was used to extend the growing season for apples.

In the 1970s, studies showed that alar could cause cancer. In 1977, the EPA began testing it. In 1985, the EPA said that alar should be banned as a health threat.

But the EPA also said that there should be more studies. Alar was left on the market until more tests were completed in the 1990s.

Meanwhile, a 1988 study of alar was done on children aged two to five by the Natural Resources Defense Council. This study showed that alar was harmful to children, who eat seven times as many apples and drink eighteen times as much apple juice as the average woman, according to the council.

These results made some schools stop serving apples, while some parents threw apples and juices away. Negative news reports about the risks of alar in 1989 cost apple growers over $100 million in apple sales that year. Apple growers and the EPA claimed that apples are checked for alar and that it is not used in apple sauce and juices. But the EPA did urge that the chemical be voluntarily taken off the market because it had caused cancer in test animals. The EPA aimed at banning the chemical by 1991.

There is another twist to the alar story. The maker of alar, Uniroyal Chemical Company, decided in 1989 to stop marketing the chemical in the United States. However, Uniroyal still sold it overseas. And, since 50 percent of our apple juice is imported, we continue to get traces of alar in our diet.

Since 1975, insecticide sales in this nation have leveled off because FIFRA controlled their production and sale. The pesticide industry has responded to this restriction in two ways.

THE CIRCLE OF POISON

The first response of the pesticide industry to FIFRA has been an effort to increase sales overseas, especially in

The major types of insecticides.

TYPE	EXAMPLES	PERSISTENCE
Chlorinated hydrocarbons	DDT, aldrin, dieldrin, endrin, heptachlor, toxaphene, lindane, chlordane, kepone, DDE	High (2 to 15 years)
Organophosphates	Malathion, parathion, diazinon	Low to moderate (1 to 12 weeks, or a few years)
Carbamates	Sevin, Baygon, aldicarb	Usually low (up to 2 weeks)

developing countries. According to "The Circle of Poison," by David Weir and Mark Schapiro, many American chemical companies use developing countries as markets for pesticides that cannot be legally sold here. Such companies, with factories in North America and Europe, distribute pesticides too hazardous for general use in the United States. These chemical companies own farms in underdeveloped countries. The governments of those countries pay the chemical companies for the pesticides, which are sprayed in the fields by workers paid a meager wage.

Pesticides in such nations are deadly weapons. First of all, their use is not controlled by laws. Second, workers are not trained in how to apply them properly. Third, the workers cannot read the directions and warnings on the labels, because they are printed in the language of the country where the chemicals were made. African and Asian workers commonly use pesticides with labels printed in German. Central and South American workers use chemicals with English labels.

The labels include few directions or warnings, as required by FIFRA in the United States. The companies supervising the spraying programs do not issue masks or other protective gear to workers. The workers inhale, touch, and even swallow large doses of whatever they are spraying.

The pesticides enter the irrigation canals that are often the only sources of household water for the workers. As a result, the people wash their clothing and eating utensils in water contaminated with toxic pesticides.

But people in the rich nations are the victims, too. Pesticide exports really do create "a circle of poison." They disable workers in North American chemical factories that produce them. And these pesticides later return to us in the food we import from poor nations.

In 1976, for instance, our government refused to accept 500,000 pounds of DDT-contaminated beef from El Salvador. Some of this meat contained nineteen times the amount of pesticides allowed by the EPA at that time. And nearly half the coffee beans imported into the United States are contaminated with pesticides produced here but banned from use here.

In 1989, 40 percent of the 1.5 billion pounds of pesticides produced in the United States were sold to

Pesticides found in imported coffee beans (1974–1977).

COUNTRY OF ORIGIN	NUMBER OF SAMPLES TAKEN	NUMBER WITH PESTICIDES
Angola (Africa)	1	1
Brazil (South America)	2	2
Colombia (South America)	21	5
Costa Rica (Central America)	2	0
Dominican Republic (Caribbean)	1	0
Ecuador (South America)	10	6
El Salvador (Central America)	2	1
Guatemala (Central America)	5	2
Haiti (Caribbean)	1	1
Honduras (Central America)	2	1
India (Asia)	4	4
Indonesia (Asia)	1	1
Ivory Coast (Africa)	2	1
Kenya (Africa)	1	0

(continued on next page)

COUNTRY OF ORIGIN	NUMBER OF SAMPLES TAKEN	NUMBER WITH PESTICIDES
Mexico (Central America)	5	4
New Guinea (South Pacific)	2	1
Nicaragua (Central America)	2	0
Panama (Central America)	1	0
Peru (South America)	5	2
Rwanda (Africa)	1	1
Uganda (Africa)	1	1
Venezuela (South America)	2	1
Total (22)	**74**	**35**

Percentage contaminated: 47.3%
Pesticides detected: DDT, DDE, BHC, lindane, dieldrin, heptachlor, diazinon, malathion

foreign nations. Of that amount, 25 percent were registered for use here. The registration of another 31 million pounds of pesticides shipped overseas had been canceled by the EPA.

Many of these pesticides have not been completely tested for their effects on human health or the environment. Others, like DDT, are known to cause cancer, mutations, and birth defects. Yet FIFRA allows banned or unregistered pesticides to be exported.

You might think the poor nations are using these pesticides to grow food crops for their hungry people. This is not so. The pesticides are more often used on export crops, because the North American people demand blemish-free products. These include bananas, coffee, tea, tapioca, strawberries, peppers, and tomatoes.

In 1984, the Food and Drug Administration (FDA) tested imported coffee for signs of pesticides banned in the United States. High levels of these pesticides on imported food are illegal, but enforcement is weak. Each year, the FDA samples less than 1 percent of imported foods for pesticide contamination. And only 3 percent of the foods found to be contaminated are not sold.

In 1983, the United Nations called for restrictions on the export of banned products. Only the United States opposed this resolution. President Reagan said that nations receiving banned chemicals from the United States should be free to use them if they wish. He said that if United States companies don't sell them these chemicals, someone else will.

Yet the problem is not rich countries taking advantage of poor countries. Most people in both rich and poor countries are victims of the circle of poison. The differences in our standards of living hide our similarities. We are all subject to the activities of a few companies and governments that influence the lives of people worldwide.

In some cases, the public is challenging the use of pesticides and other farm chemicals. An end to the era of chemical control in farming may be near. If people keep demanding fruits and vegetables with no detectable traces of pesticides, and if new chemical-free farming methods are not developed, the result for farmers could be billions of dollars in lost sales.

Many farmers are now looking for ways to cut down on their use of pesticides. Various "teaching farms" around the country have helped farmers find energy-saving ways to reduce these uses and thus lower their costs. In fact, some experts claim that we could cut pesticide use by 35 to 50 percent and still maintain our current crop yields. They say there would be no loss of pest control.

In 1988, the EPA classified more than 70 of the 360 pesticide ingredients that are allowed to be used on food as possible human carcinogens. New studies indicate that other chemicals are hazardous. So the EPA is gradually restricting the use of more pesticides. In many other cases, manufacturers are withdrawing their products for use on vegetables and fruit crops because they say it is too costly to conduct safety studies on such products.

The new information awakened the public and scared farmers. Consumers were fearful of the health perils and distrusted the chemical companies who said the products were safe. Thus, people are demanding that both fresh and processed foods have no detectable levels of pesticides.

There is no question that we have produced much from our land. But the question lingers: in return for all these farm products, have we paid too high a price? Farming with chemicals affects soil fertility. It affects the purity of our groundwater. It affects the health of our farm workers and the vitality of our farming communities.

But we are not without choices. Our values determine what is produced and what sells. If we value farming with few or no chemicals, we can show that through our buying habits. Meanwhile, some commonsense steps can help you reduce your risk from pesticides:

1. Completely rinse and scrub (with a brush) fruits and vegetables. If possible, peel them.

2. Remove and discard outer leaves of leafy vegetables, such as lettuce and cabbage.

3. Eat a varied diet so no single food or its contents dominates your diet.

4. Choose in-season, locally grown products. The closer to home they are grown, the less likely they are to carry pesticides to prevent spoilage during shipping.

In the near future, the fossil fuels from which farm chemicals are made will start running out. As this happens, we will have to return to an agricultural system of growing food rather than an agrichemical system. But will we be ready for it?

AN EXPERIMENT

A Toxicology Test

Get any two liquid pesticide products. Wear gloves and a mask when handling them. Then buy some living water fleas, known as *Daphnia,* from a pet store. If the store has none, ask your teacher to get some. These are not real fleas. They are cousins to shrimp and crayfish.

Set up three 100-milliliter plastic cups. Label them A, B, and C. Fill the first with distilled water. Fill the second with 90 percent distilled water and 10 percent pesticide number one. Fill the third with 90 percent distilled water and 10 percent pesticide number two.

Using a medicine dropper, place two water fleas in each cup. Observe and record their behavior for ten minutes. Record the time that any cease moving.

In which cup do the water fleas move fastest for the longest time? In which cup, if any, do they stay near or on the bottom? In which cup do they stop moving first? Thus, which pesticide seems most toxic?

Try this experiment again, using different pesticide concentrations. Try, for example, a solution made up of 70 percent distilled water and 30 percent pesticide. Do the results differ from before? Why, or why not? Record all your observations in your notebook.

CHAPTER 8:
HERBICIDES AND DIOXIN

In Chapter 7, we saw that FIFRA controlled the production and sale of insecticides in this country, but that the chemical industry reacted by selling more insecticides overseas. The industry also reacted to the decrease in domestic sales of insecticides by trying to sell more herbicides. Herbicides, or defoliants, are chemicals that kill weeds and other troublesome plants. They do this by causing the cell walls to take up water at a faster rate than normal, producing elongation in the stem, little or no root growth, and leaves that have less chlorophyll. This kills the plant.

The herbicide market is booming, with sales of several billion dollars a year. But these plant poisons, too, cause environmental problems.

Two of the most widely used herbicides are 2,4-D and 2,4,5-T. These two chemicals are biodegradable. Still, 2,4,5-T has caused serious problems. Its safety has been questioned for some time, and problems from it have occurred in places thousands of miles apart.

Millions of pounds of 2,4,5-T have been sprayed throughout the United States. It has been used along power lines and next to highways and railroads. This chemical was also sprayed annually on millions of acres of national forests by the U.S. Forest Service. This was done to kill low-lying shrubs and give evergreens more sunlight.

Ranchers west of the Mississippi River used 2,4,5-T to kill scrub trees that interfered with grazing cattle. Rice growers in Missouri, Arkansas, and Mississippi used a highly diluted form of the chemical on many acres to kill weeds. The rice farmers say that the diluted chemical will not harm the rice or the people who eat the rice.

As early as the late 1940s, tests showed that 2,4,5-T was possibly quite toxic. The chemical industry ignored these findings. Government studies in the 1960s linked low levels of 2,4,5-T to birth defects in rats and mice. The results of these studies were kept secret until 1969.

These results, along with pressure from environmental experts, caused the U.S. Department of Agriculture to restrict the use of 2,4,5-T in 1970. The herbicide was not allowed in household products. Nor could it be used near lakes, parks, recreation areas, or homes.

But these restrictions affected only 20 percent of all 2,4,5-T used in North America. More than a million pounds are still legally being used each year on forest shrubs, livestock grazing land, rice fields, and brush along rights-of-way.

THE OREGON COAST

Oregon has many forests from which lumber companies harvest fir trees. Ever since World War II, when 2,4,5-T was first developed, these companies have sprayed it on the forests in Oregon.

People living near the forests began having problems. According to Allen Boraiko, eight women in Oregon had eleven miscarriages between 1973 and 1977. All eleven miscarriages followed spraying of nearby forests with 2,4,5-T. At other times, when no spraying was done, the same women had normal full-term pregnancies. Pregnant women who moved into the region just before spraying time had miscarriages.

The women's doctors could not explain the miscarriages. So, in 1978, the women asked the EPA to investigate. The EPA looked at the test results from ten years earlier. It also compared the miscarriage data from coastal Oregon with data from the rest of Oregon.

In 1979, the EPA temporarily banned the use of 2,4,5-T and a related herbicide on forests and rights-of-way nationwide. Scientists had known for a decade that 2,4,5-T caused birth defects in animals. Yet the EPA did not act until effects on humans were found. Meanwhile, 2,4,5-T was approved for use on ranchlands and rice fields.

Despite this knowledge of birth defects, the timber industry, Dow Chemical, and ten other herbicide makers fought the ban in court. They claimed the EPA's study was not scientific. But, in 1979, they lost. Dow Chemical was the chief manufacturer of 2,4,5-T, which contains a toxic substance called dioxin.

DIOXIN

Dioxin is the name given to a family of 75 compounds, not all of which are toxic. The kind of dioxin found in 2,4,5-T is called TCDD. It kills lab animals in doses as low as a few parts per billion. TCDD is a chlorinated dioxin and is one of the most toxic chemicals known.

TCDD has played a major role in some of our worst environmental disasters. At Love Canal, it was one of the chemicals in the runoff from the abandoned Hooker Chemical dump. In Newark, New Jersey, in 1983, TCDD was found in soil beneath a former chemical factory.

TCDD is formed as a by-product during the manufacture of 2,4,5-T. It occurs in this chemical at a concentration of up to several parts per million. It can also be formed by the burning of plastic material that contains chlorine. TCDD seems to be a cancer promoter rather than a carcinogen. Still, rats that have been fed TCDD at a level of just five parts per trillion get cancer, according to a 1983 article by D. Grady in *Discover* magazine. TCDD may also cause leukemia, kidney failure, liver and lung diseases, birth defects, and miscarriages in lab animals at low levels. There is likewise concern that TCDD, unlike 2,4,5-T, is not biodegradable. It may be biomagnifying in food webs. Soil bacteria usually decompose 2,4-D and 2,4,5-T, but not TCDD.

Studies have found biomagnification of TCDD in the fat of beef cattle grazing on sprayed land. And if rats can get cancer after being fed dioxin at only five parts per trillion, the amount of TCDD in the American diet of beef could cause many deaths.

And what about cattle raised in other nations, to which North American companies export 2,4,5-T? How much TCDD contamination occurs in those people and their livestock?

AGENT ORANGE

A debate over the use of 2,4,5-T began in the 1960s during the Vietnam War. It was used in high concentrations in an herbicide called Agent Orange. This herbicide was a 50-50 mixture of 2,4-D and 2,4,5-T. Twelve million gallons (93 million pounds) of it were sprayed on five million acres of jungle in South Vietnam between 1965 and 1970. The jungle had been a natural hideout for enemy soldiers. Agent Orange exposed enemy troops by killing the jungle plants in which they hid.

But public pressure against the spraying was great, because 2.4 million American soldiers also were exposed to Agent Orange. The herbicides used in Vietnam were several times more powerful than the strongest ones allowed in this country.

The Agent Orange story was first made public in 1978. Since then, thousands of veterans have filed claims with the U.S. Veterans Administration (VA) for disability

American Air Force C-123s spraying Agent Orange in South Vietnam in May 1967.
Photo courtesy U.S. Air Force

payments based on exposure to Agent Orange. Such disabilities include liver damage, loss of appetite or weight, muscle weakness, certain forms of cancer, nerve damage in arms or legs, sleep and mood problems, a severe skin rash called chloracne, and birth defects in their children. Vietnamese people claim similar problems.

Both the Defense Department and the VA, however, deny that such problems are due to exposure to Agent Orange. A recent study done by the Centers for Disease Control in Atlanta, Georgia, also shows no clear-cut relationship between veterans' disabilities and exposure to a single chemical.

By 1980, the VA was giving $48 per month in disability pay to only three Vietnam veterans for chloracne scars. This so angered other veterans that fifteen thousand of them filed a lawsuit against Dow Chemical and six other companies. In 1984, these companies agreed to set up a $180 million fund for thousands of veterans and their families. But the veterans were not satisfied with the agreement, since this amount of money, when split up evenly, would total only a few thousand dollars for each veteran. Many veterans have spent much more than this on medical bills already.

By 1989, this fund had grown to $240 million with interest. That year, payments from the fund were made to individuals, families, and social service agencies that help Vietnam veterans. About 30,000 veterans and 18,000 surviving families of veterans were eligible for payments. Some of the funds were also paid to Australian and New Zealand military people exposed to Agent Orange in Vietnam.

Also in 1989, a U.S. District judge struck down VA rules that denied Agent Orange benefits to veterans who claimed disabilities due to illnesses other than chloracne. In addition, the judge ordered the VA to reopen all claims it had previously denied under those rules.

Why are the effects of TCDD appearing only now in veterans? After all, many years have passed since they were exposed to 2,4,5-T. One possible explanation is that TCDD concentrates in fat, as it is nearly insoluble in water. There it stays until the person loses weight. Then the fat breaks down, releasing the dioxin to cause illness. Dioxin's connection to birth defects might be caused by its molecular resemblance to other mutagenic chemicals.

How dioxin may cause illness even after many years.

Spraying of jungle	→ U.S. troops drink contaminated water and sleep on contaminated soil	→ TCDD remains in fat	→ Dieting veteran loses some fat years later	→ TCDD is released into blood, traveling to body organs until it gets into fat cells again

THE VETERANS ADMINISTRATION AND DIOXIN STUDIES

To date, there is no scientific proof that the health problems of Vietnam veterans are connected with Agent Orange. In 1979, Congress told the VA to start scientific studies of veterans. But the VA did not make much progress.

Veterans nationwide accused the VA of delaying its own studies. If studies showed a connection between Agent Orange and illness, the veterans could collect millions of dollars in disability benefits.

It is hard to detect how much TCDD or any other chlorinated dioxin is in a human. Until recently, no test could reliably measure small TCDD levels. What is more, many years have passed since veterans were exposed. So TCDD should be even harder to find. Although the chemical can be measured in fat samples, these must be taken surgically.

In 1981, a method was found to detect tiny amounts of TCDD in the blood, even of people exposed to the chemical years before. In 1985, a test using this method was begun in New Jersey in an attempt to link levels of dioxin in veterans and nonveterans with certain disorders. Blood samples were taken from fifty Vietnam veterans who were heavily exposed to Agent Orange. Other blood samples were taken from fifty Vietnam veterans who were not heavily exposed. Fifty veterans who did not serve in Vietnam were used as controls in the study. Blood samples were taken from them as well. The results of this study were mixed. Levels of TCDD were found in the blood of some exposed veterans, but not all. The results are not clear. Further studies, with more people, are needed.

DIOXIN AND PAPER MILLS

EPA scientists suspected a link between paper pulp mills and dioxin in 1980. In 1983, fish caught downstream from several pulp mills in Wisconsin contained high levels (50 ppt) of dioxin. Other studies done on streams in other states confirmed these results in 1989.

In the pulp bleaching process, chlorine forms toxic chlorine-based compounds, including dioxin. This means that all bleached paper products could be contaminated with dioxin. These products include coffee filters, toilet paper, paper cups, paper plates, disposable diapers, and milk cartons. A recent study found traces of dioxin in milk that had been stored in cartons.

In 104 of the nation's 600 paper mills, chlorinated compounds are released into the air and water when wastes are dumped. Each mill releases thirty-five to fifty tons of chlorinated chemicals each day.

Up to 1,000 different chlorinated compounds are formed during bleaching. Among the 300 compounds that have been identified, many are carcinogens that are controlled by federal laws when they come from chemical factories but not when they are discharged by the pulp industry.

The EPA has not produced rules to get rid of dioxin contamination of air, water, and paper products. Instead, in 1988, the EPA studied the 104 paper mills again, agreeing to finish the study by 1990. But even after that is done, the EPA can take another year to write regulations.

Meanwhile, Sweden has banned the sale of chlorine-bleached disposable diapers. Austrians use unbleached brown coffee filters and milk cartons. Swedish mills bleach their pulp with oxygen-based chemicals.

The North American pulp industry resists requests for chlorine-free and unbleached paper products. Coffee filter makers claim that they don't have enough unbleached pulp. Yet unbleached pulp is cheaper and easier to make. The pulp industry is expanding to produce more chlorine-bleached pulp. Why? To satisfy our demand for white paper products that look cleaner than unbleached products.

TIMES BEACH

One town that suffered from dioxin contamination was Times Beach, Missouri. The town began in the 1920s as a recreational area on the Meramec River. By 1983, it had a population of 2,400 and 800 homes. It ceased to exist in 1984. What happened?

In 1971, Russell Bliss had a business in Times Beach; he removed waste oil from service stations and chemicals from factories all over northeastern Missouri. Unknown to Bliss, the oil mixture was contaminated with TCDD from a factory that produced herbicides. Bliss used a mixture of the waste oils to spray on horse arenas, stables, streets, parking lots, and farms throughout the state to keep the dust down.

Within days after spraying two show grounds, horses, birds, and other animals in those areas died. A child who had played in one area became very ill. State officials investigated. In 1974, the problems were traced to TCDD. Contaminated soil was removed from one site. State officials thought dioxin decayed quickly and that no more action was necessary.

But people around the areas kept complaining of persistent chemical odors. The areas were cleaned twice by the time the EPA again took samples from them in 1981. These samples showed TCDD levels up to 1,800 ppb. The grounds were shut down in 1982.

Also in 1982, the EPA was called to Times Beach to measure dioxin levels in soil and streets flooded by the river. The levels here were found to be more than 100 ppb, one hundred times the level thought to be harmful for long-term contact. So the EPA recommended moving people out of the town.

The federal and Missouri state governments bought the town for $36.7 million in 1983. They also paid to move the people to nearby towns. Up to now, the state government has "officially" found twenty-six places in Missouri that are contaminated with TCDD. But the final total may be more than seventy-five. Dozens of other towns in Oregon, Ohio, and other states are also affected by dioxin.

Meanwhile, the EPA does not know how to decontaminate the town of Times Beach. Bacteria do not decompose TCDD. Radiation and high-temperature burning are not practical for treating tons of soil. As for Bliss, the man who spread the poison, he was not brought to trial. He was questioned by state and federal officials and found to be innocent of any purposeful wrongdoing.

In 1986, 128 residents of Times Beach and other Missouri areas sued over dioxin contamination. They got a $19 million settlement from the company that failed to clean up the contaminated waste oil before it was to be used.

The EPA had thought that dioxins easily move through soil. This would make disposal of dioxin-contaminated soil and waste on land very hazardous. But in 1986, a study showed that dioxin seems to move in soil slowly. The rate of movement is perhaps only one inch in 400 years. If this is true, the EPA hopes to dispose of soils containing low amounts of dioxin in abandoned mines.

CONCLUSIONS

These chemical tragedies bring up some questions. On whom should we place the blame? Must human damage be done before a chemical is banned? Should a company have to prove beyond all doubt that its products will not make us all unwilling test animals in the largest of all laboratories—the world?

You will see in Chapter 9 that these same questions apply to other deadly chemicals as well.

AN EXPERIMENT

Effects of Herbicides on Plants

Buy some green pea seeds from a garden supply store. Also get two liquid herbicides, sterile soil, and three plastic flower pots. You will also need a ruler, adhesive tape, distilled water, and three 1,000-milliliter beakers. Remember to wash your hands thoroughly after handling the herbicides. Be careful not to get them in your eyes.

Plant four seeds in each pot of sterile soil, about one inch below the soil surface. Label the pots A, B, and C with adhesive tape.

Keep the pots in partial sunlight during the day. Over the next two weeks or so, water all three pots every day with 20 milliliters of distilled water. Do this until the seedlings push through the soil surface and grow their first two leaves. Not all the seeds will sprout. Record how many do in each pot.

Make a solution of one herbicide by pouring 900 milliliters of distilled water into a beaker, and adding 5 milliliters of herbicide. Stir well. Label this beaker Herbicide A Solution. Do the same with the other herbicide in another beaker. Label it Herbicide B Solution. Pour 1,000 milliliters of distilled water into the third beaker. Label it Distilled Water.

Now water pot A with 20 milliliters of Herbicide A Solution. Do this each day for two more weeks. Water pot B with 20 milliliters of Herbicide B Solution for the same length of time. Keep watering pot C with distilled water. This pot is the control.

Every three days, measure the height of each seedling with a ruler. Keep separate records for each pot. Also note any seedlings that die during the two weeks.

Which seedlings die? Which pot shows the best growth? the least growth?

CHAPTER 9:
PCBs AND PBBs

In 1981, construction workers in San Francisco accidentally broke a natural gas main. The gas spurted into the air. Since authorities feared an explosion, they moved people out of the area. After sealing the break, workers found that the gas was mixed with lubricating oil. This oil was contaminated with polychlorinated biphenyls (PCBs).

WHAT ARE PCBs?

PCBs are mixtures of some seventy chlorinated hydrocarbons. From 1929 to 1979, PCBs were used as insulating fluids in electrical transformers because they are heat resistant. They were also used in the production of ink, adhesives, copying paper, wall coverings, television sets, and lubricating oil.

About 1.4 billion pounds of PCBs have been made in North America. Of this amount, 450 million pounds are now in the environment. Another 750 million pounds are still in use, and some of them will slowly enter the environment because PCBs are persistent. They do not biodegrade, and they are fat soluble, so they biomagnify through food webs.

PCBs are found all over the world. Wherever old electrical equipment has been dumped, it may leak PCBs into water. The toxics are absorbed by plants. PCBs biomagnify in fish that take them in from the water and eat the plants that contain them. Mammals that eat the PCB-laden fish are at great risk.

LAB TESTS

PCBs were tested on rats to see if they cause cancer. Rats were fed 100 ppm of PCBs in their diet for twenty-one months. About 14 percent developed some type of cancer; most had liver cancer. Among the 173 control animals, the ones who were not fed any PCBs, only one—less than 1 percent—developed any cancers.

More bad news resulted from monkey experiments. Two groups of adult female monkeys were fed PCBs in their diets for six months. One group's dose was 5 ppm; the other's was 2.5 ppm. They were then mated with males kept on normal diets.

Of the eight females fed 5 ppm of PCBs, five had miscarriages. Two others did not become pregnant. Only one gave birth. Of the eight females fed 2.5 ppm, five gave birth to very tiny infants, and three had miscarriages. The six babies nursed for four months. Three babies died during this period. The others showed chloracne, abnormally high activity, and problems in learning simple tasks. It took only three months for the nursing babies to reach the same contamination levels as their mothers.

EFFECT ON HUMAN BABIES

The PCB tests showed that future generations of human beings would be tainted with one of the most toxic and long-lasting synthetic organic chemicals ever created. Research also showed that nursing human infants get higher concentrations of PCBs than those that exist in their mothers. Why should this be so?

Like any other female mammal that produces milk, a human mother has nutrients stored in her fat cells. PCBs build up in those cells. Once the PCBs get into the blood, they rapidly get into her milk. Since infants feed almost exclusively on milk, each feeding increases the amount of PCBs in the small systems of the infants. The same is true for any toxic chemical that is persistent, insoluble in water, soluble in fat, and capable of biomagnifying. Even DDT is still found in human mother's milk because of its persistence in the environment.

Mother's milk is more nutritious than cow's milk. But the average PCB levels in human milk are seven times greater than the amount the government permits in cow's milk. Cow's milk also has a much greater PCB level than the food the cows have eaten. A milk substitute is the only other choice to feed a baby.

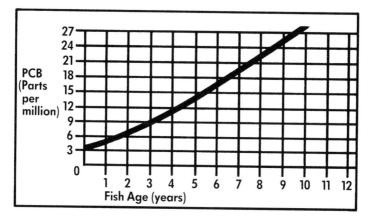

The levels of PCBs in trout in comparison to their age.
Notice that the older the fish, the more PCBs it has.
People usually eat older fish, since such fish are larger.

We do not yet know the long-term effects of PCBs on people. EPA studies show the number of Americans with PCBs increased from 1972 to 1981. Since then, the numbers have declined. But infants of women who ate Lake Michigan fish contaminated with PCBs show learning problems, according to current research.

Various incidents link PCBs with chloracne, headaches, nausea, diarrhea, loss of hair, fatigue, numbness, liver problems, cancer, birth defects, and dark skin coloring beneath the fingernails and in the gums.

INDUSTRY AND GOVERNMENT

By 1970, there was much concern over contamination of the environment with PCBs. Monsanto Chemical Company said it would sell PCBs only for use in items that would not release them into the environment. Soon after this, PCB levels in some rivers decreased. However, PCBs were still placed in transformers.

In 1975, New York State warned people about eating salmon and bass from the Hudson River and Lake Ontario. Fish had been found with up to 350 ppm of PCBs, 175 times the level considered safe by the EPA.

Where were the PCBs in the Hudson River and Lake Ontario coming from? Two General Electric factories on the river had federal permits to release waste PCBs into it. They had been doing so since 1946. General Electric was found guilty by the New York State Department of Conservation of disobeying state water-quality laws. About 500,000 pounds of PCBs are still in the Hudson, mostly upriver. Several thousand pounds move downstream a few miles each year.

In 1976, the state and General Electric agreed on a settlement. The company gave $3 million toward a $6 million Hudson River cleanup program. It also gave another one million dollars toward the search for other chemicals to replace PCBs.

In 1979, the United States stopped producing and importing PCBs. This decision came more than ten years after Japan had banned them. Monsanto had ceased manufacturing them in 1977.

Despite this legal ban, however, PCBs know no political boundaries. Their concentrations in the body increase as more of them are eaten. Most other nations that make PCBs still have not banned their production.

The EPA has required the removal of PCBs from all

electrical transformers in U.S. apartment and office buildings, hospitals, and malls by 1990. Also banned is the further installation of PCB-filled transformers in or near commercial buildings. This will still leave 140,000 sealed electrical transformers containing some 375,000 tons of PCBs. Each year, PCBs are released into the environment as these transformers leak, catch fire, or explode.

Disposing of PCBs is never easy. But scientists have found that cancer-causing PCBs can be broken down by microbes. In the absence of oxygen, certain bacteria called *anaerobic* bacteria thrive. These can break down PCB molecules into other molecules with removed or rearranged chlorine atoms.

Once changed, the chemicals are thought to be less harmful. They may be degraded further by the more abundant *aerobic* bacteria that thrive in water that is rich in oxygen.

Anaerobic bacteria are found in mud sediments beneath rivers. The breakdown of PCBs by anaerobic bacteria works best when high PCB concentrations are present—about 700 ppm.

Of course, high-temperature burning and chemical methods have been developed to destroy PCBs. But many experts believe that biological destroyers are cheaper, safer, and more effective.

The idea of breeding microbes to destroy pollutants is simple. At waste dumps, microbes are gathered that may have already developed an ability to degrade chemicals. These bacteria are next placed in glass dishes that often have large amounts of pollutants. The bacteria may be deprived of their normal nutrients in such dishes, known as *cultures.* The bacteria, faced with this choice, either develop a taste for pollutants or die of starvation. Most or all of the bacteria may die in such conditions. But a few sometimes adapt to their harsh environment and survive. These are then reproduced to produce new types, or *strains.*

The harmless microbes that are used in the process are common in ordinary soil. But use of the method is complicated because bacteria that have been developed to attack one chemical may be totally incapable of coping with a closely related chemical.

The destruction of PCBs is especially difficult because no single bacteria can degrade PCBs. So scientists try to develop groups of several types of bacteria to work together. It is difficult to match up the right strains of bacteria with the exact PCBs they can degrade. But together, anaerobic and aerobic bacteria might clean the PCBs from the Hudson River. To speed up this process, General Electric is studying ways to get nutrients down to the bacteria on the river bottom.

THE TOXIC SUBSTANCES CONTROL ACT

The public was angered at the news that General Electric had contaminated the Hudson River. People showed their anger by fighting for Congress to pass the 1976 Toxic Substances Control Act (TOSCA). This law was meant to control the nearly 1,000 new industrial chemicals entering the market each year.

As part of TOSCA, the EPA listed 45,000 chemicals being made in America. Any substance not on this list is a new chemical. A company must tell the EPA at least ninety days before starting production of a new chemical. The EPA may want to test this chemical for its safety. If so, the agency can block production for up to 180 days.

Environmental groups consider TOSCA important in keeping track of hazardous substances. But these groups are worried because Congress has not provided enough funds for the EPA to enforce TOSCA.

The chemical companies are also worried about the law. It requires them to give the EPA information about new chemicals. This information, in other words, can no longer be kept secret; it must be made available to the EPA and thus to competing companies as well. Companies will also have to spend more time and money to test new chemicals for toxicity. They feel these tests are unnecessary, according to an article by R.D. Zentner in *Ecolibrium.*

xxxxxEnvironmental groups, however, claim the EPA does not vigorously enforce TOSCA. Of the 1,000 new chemicals produced each year, the EPA has excused many from full testing. It has rejected the production of only a few.

In fact, the EPA has not begun actual testing of new chemicals under TOSCA, because of questions about the amount and type of testing that should be done. At best, testing will be costly and time-consuming. Even then, any data gained from testing will be questionable: most tests are done on animals, and not all chemicals that are harmful to animals are risky for people.

Suppose industry gets EPA permission to make a new product. No EPA rules tell it how to sell, use, or discard the product. The company is also free to give the new product a trade name that does not tell the buyer what chemicals are in it. Thus, neither the worker who makes it nor the public who buys and uses it knows what is in it. Nor is the company required to tell us what hazards it may have. The following story, told by Donald Maclean in his book entitled *PBB: The Poisoning of Michigan,* is a tragic but true example of what can happen when such safeguards are not required by a government agency.

A TOXIC MIX-UP

Michigan Chemical Company in St. Louis, Michigan, was the largest maker of polybrominated biphenyls (PBBs). The chemical characteristics of PBBs make them resistant to fire.

In 1971, this company produced a PBB product useful in putting out fires. It was called Firemaster. The company enforced no rules for its safe handling by workers. By 1972, many workers who handled Firemaster had memory losses and were often very tired.

In 1973, the company made a cattle-feed product that, when mixed with grain, made the feed more nutritious. This product was called Nutrimaster. Its largest buyer was

Farm Bureau Services (FBS), connected with the Michigan Farm Bureau.

Firemaster was shipped in brown bags with red-stenciled labels. Nutrimaster was shipped in brown bags with blue-stenciled labels. Both products were stored in the same warehouse. In 1973, during a paper shortage, the company decided to package both chemicals in identical bags, with the names of both products stenciled in black. In the warehouse, a handler accidentally shipped forty bags of Firemaster to the FBS mill in Battle Creek. There, in 1974, it was mixed with cattle feed and sent to dozens of farms.

Shortly thereafter, cows refused to eat or give milk. They aborted their calves. The cows had kidney problems, humped backs, overgrown hooves, and damaged udders. Dairy farmers tried to convince the state department of agriculture that something was wrong with the feed. The state disagreed. Then one farmer had a scientist from the federal agriculture department test the feed. PBBs were found in it.

But by this time, eleven months had passed. Other Michigan farms had become contaminated. They were now quarantined. Many people had eaten contaminated meat, eggs, milk, butter, and cheese. Of over one thousand people examined from throughout Michigan, 37 percent had liver disorders, memory loss, fatigue, numbness, dizziness, headaches, skin and stomach problems, hair loss, and unusual nails.

In 1975, the quarantined farmers were paid by the state to destroy millions of chickens, thousands of sheep, over thirty thousand cows, and six thousand pigs. They did this to prevent the poisoning of still more people. The animals were buried in special landfills.

The state filed a $120 million lawsuit against the Michigan Chemical Company, now known as the Velsicol Chemical Company. Farmers also filed 650 claims against Velsicol, totaling $40 million.

PBB production was finally banned in America in 1977. But costs of the tragedy are still being tallied. PBBs have been found in cow's milk and in that of nursing human mothers. It is in meat, in water supplies, and in the bodies of most people in Michigan. PBB's ability to cause cancer was confirmed in 1981 by the National Toxicology Program, a government agency.

This unfortunate incident would not have occurred if we had had a strong toxic substances control act at the time. Michigan Chemical would not have been allowed to make a feed chemical and toxic substances on the same site. Nor would the company have been allowed to use such similar brand names, or to package the chemicals in the same type of bag.

THE TOXIC CLEANUP

How did Velsicol Chemical Company clean up the remaining PBBs from its factory site? In 1982, the EPA

A dairy farmer in Michigan with a champion Holstein that ate contaminated feed. The cow had to be destroyed.

Photo, AP/Wide World

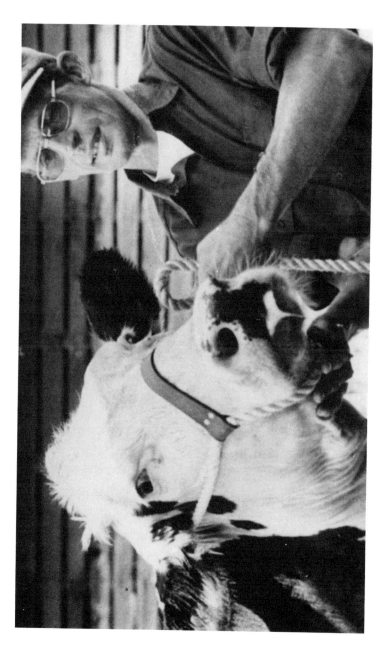

settled with the company out of court. Velsicol agreed to clean up four dumps containing PBBs on its property. The cleanup cost the company $38.5 million. In return, the EPA and the state agreed to drop all present and future claims against Velsicol, including the $120 million and $40 million lawsuits.

Under the terms of the 1976 Resource Conservation and Recovery Act (see Chapter 10), the EPA could have cleaned the waste sites itself, then charged Velsicol for costs. But the government instead made an agreement with Velsicol to force the company to clean up the sites.

Velsicol buried its PBBs in a deep well, sealed with clay. The company is responsible for checking the site for leakage over the next thirty years.

But the well is near a river that runs into Lake Huron. Environmental groups fear leakage of PBBs into the river and groundwater.

AN EXPERIMENT

Cleaning Up an Oil Spill

Many lubricating oils in electrical transformers still have PCBs in them. As utility companies discard old transformers, some oil (and PCBs) may spill. This activity will show you how hard it is to clean up an oil spill.

You will need three flat dishes, masking tape, tap water, used motor oil, an eyedropper, plastic cups, baking soda, grass, paper towels, liquid detergent, flour, ice, cotton, and a graduated cylinder.

Label three dishes A, B, and C. Add 10 milliliters of water to each dish. Then add 10 drops of motor oil to each dish. Your task is to remove the oil from the water.

Try to take the oil out of dish A using plastic cups, grass, and baking soda. First place a few grass blades on the surface of the liquid in dish A. Then measure out five milliliters of baking soda in a graduated cylinder, and add that to the dish. Both grass and baking soda should absorb some of the oil. Measure the remaining volume of liquid, using the graduated cylinder.

Try removing the oil from dish B with an eyedropper, paper towel, and detergent. First, observe how much liquid you can absorb with a paper towel. Then add five milliliters of detergent. Measure the remaining volume of liquid as before.

Try to remove the oil from dish C with flour, then ice, and finally cotton.

Which set of materials is most effective? Least effective? Can you give reasons for your answers?

Record all your findings in your notebook.

CHAPTER 10:
CONTROLLING DISPOSAL OF HAZARDOUS SUBSTANCES

Every process for producing useful things also produces materials that are not useful. These useless substances may be by-products of the production process. They may be leftover raw materials that have served their purpose.

Most of these wastes are harmless. Rice straw, for example, is difficult for a farmer to remove from his fields. Yet it is not hazardous, for it readily decomposes in the soil.

But certain wastes are dangerous, because they do not easily decay. The manufactured product itself may be harmful. For example, unused pesticides left over after spraying a field are as dangerous as those sprayed on the field. If allowed to biomagnify, they may become more concentrated in the bodies of certain members of a food chain.

More than 890 million pounds of hazardous wastes are generated each year. This includes 235 million pounds of carcinogens and 527 million pounds of nerve poisons.

Today, thousands of uncontrolled hazardous waste sites across the nation require cleanup. Experts estimate the cost of cleaning them could be billions of dollars. Chemical waste accounts for at least 71 percent of this hazardous waste. How can we gain control of this problem?

METHODS OF DISPOSAL

One way to handle hazardous waste is to set up central points for treatment and disposal. A waste disposal industry has already developed nationwide. The companies are paid to dispose of substances any way they can. Some of them carelessly dump chemicals into the ground, sewers, or rivers—even along highways. Government agencies have not effectively supervised their activities.

Several waste companies do their jobs well. They recycle the contents of waste barrels or burn them at high temperatures. Then they place the remains in drums in specially designed *secured landfills.*

These secured landfills are located on firm clay ground. Additional clay is put on the bottom. The landfill is then lined with a plastic sheet reinforced with nylon to prevent leakage. Such companies place all drums containing one type of chemical in one corner, while barrels filled with other wastes are placed elsewhere. This system prevents hazardous chemical reactions if different wastes mix.

Workers at the Kin Buc Landfill in Edison, New Jersey, decontaminating hazardous waste.

Photo, New Jersey Newsphotos

The Valley of the Drums in the rolling countryside near Lexington, Kentucky, in 1979.

Photo, Courier Journal *and* Louisville Times

When the dump is full, the top is graded with clay and soil in such a way that rain cannot enter the burial site. Finally, grass is planted on top to reduce erosion. Some of these landfills contain up to 350,000 barrels of waste.

But are these landfills really secure? No matter how well kept, certain toxic chemicals will remain long after we are gone. No matter how good the clay sides and bottom, nobody can guarantee the landfill will not leak. In some places, drums are recklessly dumped into these landfills. The plastic liner is broken by their metal rims. Most substances used for linings are biodegradable and will disintegrate eventually. Also, clay is not completely impermeable to water.

Unfortunately, few disposal companies use secure landfills. A common practice is to collect enough drums to fill several acres, then dump the waste and abandon it. The industries may have paid for waste treatment, but all too often it is not done.

DEEP-WELL INJECTION

In deep-well injection, liquid wastes are pumped underground through tubes into rock formations several hundred to several thousand feet deep. After passage of the Clean Water Act of 1977, many industries began injecting liquid wastes into disposal wells deep underground. By 1989, there were 120,000 such wells, with 5,000 more being added each year.

The safety of these wells is debated. Some people in government and industry say it is the best way to dispose of chemical and radioactive waste. It is far better than landfills. It is also more economical than burning the waste.

Critics, however, claim the material is put where nobody can keep track of it. They also say wastes from some wells have moved to groundwater supplies. Others have traveled back to the surface through nearby abandoned gas, oil, or water wells.

Meanwhile, the Western Research Institute in Wyoming is testing steam and hot water injection techniques.

These were originally developed for the oil drilling industry as a way to heat and move oil chemicals in soils. If heated enough, these oily wastes become less dense in water. The aim of this process is to more easily move the wastes toward a removal well.

The 1974 Safe Drinking Water Act is supposed to protect groundwater from waste injection. Likewise, since 1978 all old and new deep wells are supposed to have permits, issued by either the EPA or the states.

However, the 1974 act's rules were not developed until 1977. At that time, government economists who were fighting inflation were concerned about the cost of these rules to industry. So the EPA postponed adopting the rules until 1980. Since then, the EPA has postponed rule adoption still more; the agency says it can only prevent groundwater contamination, not clean it up.

ILLEGAL DUMPING

Still more alarming is the illegal shipment and disposal of hazardous substances. Much of this shipping and disposing is done by 15,000 chemical disposal businesses that charge thousands of dollars to industries to cart waste away. Some of these disposal companies then secretly release the material into gullies, forests, creeks, garbage landfills, sewers, lakes, even along roads.

One way to end illegal dumping would be to provide more licensed landfills. Another way would be for states to require companies to keep track of their chemicals all the way from production to disposal.

New Jersey does have such a requirement. The state uses permits to track movements of industrial wastes within its boundaries. Yet this is not totally effective. A waste hauler may say he takes the material to a disposal site outside the state. But he could really be dumping it along a road in a neighboring state. A regional permit system would help. If several neighboring states enforced the same system, it would be easier to track waste.

But to this day, neither state nor federal governments have made much of an impact on the waste problem. As the crackdown starts in one state, illegal dumping moves elsewhere, made attractive by the big money to be made and the lack of law enforcement. Today, violations even at legal disposal sites usually draw only a warning letter. The most likely illegal dumpers are small companies that cannot afford expensive pollution controls.

One person who might disagree with this is Barry Groveman, a Los Angeles attorney who heads that city's Toxic Waste Strike Force. This fifty-one-member force consists of city police, fire, sanitation, and health department staff members. Companies that dump illegally and are nabbed by the force risk jail, fines, and the shame of having to apologize for their dumping in the *Los Angeles Times*. By 1984, two years after the creation of the strike force, Groveman had put eleven L.A. executive officers behind bars. Their companies were forced to pay thousands of dollars in fines and cleanup costs.

OTHER DISPOSAL METHODS

The government could encourage hazardous-waste producers to find disposal methods that are safer than dumping. It could increase taxes of those companies that use careless disposal methods. And it could decrease taxes of those industries that try better ways of discarding wastes.

Industry can reduce hazardous waste and dispose of it safely when enticed by a savings or a profit. For example, incinerators at Dow Chemical's Louisiana factory burn toxic waste to generate steam heat and cut fuel bills. General Motors stores automaking supplies in reusable containers. This leaves fewer 55-gallon steel drums to dispose of. Allied Corporation mixes a toxic sludge with other hazardous waste to make a raw material for gases used in refrigerators. And 3M Company sells its ammonium sulfate to fertilizer makers, who change this toxic by-product of videotape manufacture into plant food. Clearly, the less waste to be gotten rid of outside the company fence, the better.

In 1988, the EPA provided money to private companies to help develop new methods for cleansing hazardous wastes and cleaning up abandoned waste sites.

One of these methods uses a combination of electrical fields and low-frequency sound waves to drive wastes out of deep soils. Another method is a filtering system: it uses dead algae that are ground to a fine powder and packed into a three-foot pipe. The algae chemically seize heavy metals like cadmium, mercury, and zinc from soil.

We also might be better off if government put as much stress on reducing and reusing waste as on regulating it. In 1981, American industry recycled only 4 percent of its toxic waste. It did this partly through waste exchanges, organizations that transfer one company's waste to another company for use as raw material. Despite the good potential of these toxic waste exchanges, since 1979 the EPA has spent almost no money to promote them. Still, by 1986 at least thirty regional waste exchanges were transferring 10 percent of the toxic wastes produced by industry.

THE RESOURCE CONSERVATION AND RECOVERY ACT

It takes the Federal government a long time to pass laws to control hazardous substances. Furthermore, once a law has been passed, the enforcement process has been bogged down with problems.

An example is the 1976 Resource Conservation and Recovery Act (RCRA). This law was passed to control disposal of newly produced toxic industrial wastes. It requires a system (1) to close toxic open dumps; (2) to count the number of waste sites; (3) to control the construction and checking of landfills; (4) to punish violators; and (5) to start a permit system for tracking hazardous wastes from production to disposal.

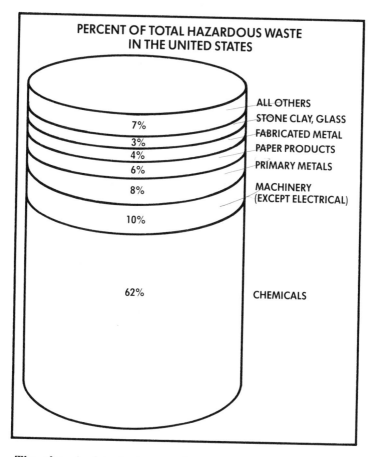

PERCENT OF TOTAL HAZARDOUS WASTE
IN THE UNITED STATES

ALL OTHERS
STONE CLAY, GLASS
FABRICATED METAL
PAPER PRODUCTS
PRIMARY METALS
MACHINERY
(EXCEPT ELECTRICAL)

7%
3%
4%
6%
8%
10%

62%   CHEMICALS

The chemical industry produces about 62 percent of industrial hazardous waste.

People who own disposal sites are required to obtain permits listing the contents and amounts of wastes they accept and the location at which each type of waste is dumped. Excused from this requirement are farmers and businesses that produce less than 100 kilograms (220 pounds) of hazardous waste each month.

These exceptions anger environmental groups. As we have seen, even small amounts of toxics can pose health hazards. Wastes that have been recycled or mixed with other products are also excused. This exception would permit a disaster like the Times Beach dioxin incident to occur again, legally, anywhere in our nation.

There were other loopholes in the RCRA. It dealt with active and future dumps, not old and abandoned sites. Covering them would have added to the cost of cleanup. Neither did the RCRA take any action against illegal dumping.

In 1984, Congress added changes to the RCRA. Land disposal of hazardous wastes was to be cut to almost zero by 1990. The EPA will allow land disposal only if a particular type of waste cannot be disposed of in some other way.

EFFECTS OF THE RCRA

One result of the RCRA was a public outcry against the establishment of new legal dump sites. Although 120 sites already existed, 100 new ones were needed right away. People protested the existing sites and would not accept new ones. Many of the 120 existing sites were under heavy pressure by the public to shut down.

Environmentalists charge that the RCRA fails to control properly many hazardous wastes. Industrialists complain that the law causes much paperwork, increases disposal costs, and threatens to cause a shortage of disposal sites.

All of this shows that efforts to solve the problem of hazardous-waste disposal by laws alone will fail. The government must also offer tax breaks for companies that come up with workable solutions.

MEDICAL WASTE

During the summers of 1987 and 1988, syringes, scalpels, vials of blood, and surgical and laboratory waste began washing up on the beaches of ten states along the Atlantic Ocean, Lake Michigan, and Lake Erie. This illegally dumped waste caused a public uproar. Beaches were closed because of the threat of hepatitis and other diseases.

As a result, Congress passed a medical waste tracking law in 1988. The law is set up much like the RCRA. It requires proper labeling and packaging of medical waste. This will protect those people who handle the material. The law also requires medical waste to be kept separate from other waste.

The law sets up a program to track ten types of medical waste from where it is produced to where it is disposed of in ten states: Connecticut, New Jersey, New York, Pennsylvania, Ohio, Indiana, Illinois, Michigan, Wisconsin, and Minnesota. Later, the program could become national if other states ask to have their medical waste monitored from production to disposal.

SUPERFUND

After the public protest against the RCRA, Congress passed another law in 1980. Nicknamed Superfund, its purpose was to speed the cleanup of our nation's most hazardous dumps.

The five-year, $1.6-billion program was designed to allow the EPA to clean the sites first and collect fines later. The agency can sue the dumpers to get back up to three times the cleanup costs. Some of the cleanup money will be raised by taxing the oil and chemical industries. The rest is coming from federal and state governments. The fund will keep growing as cleanup costs are collected.

This law also created stricter standards for handling hazardous substances. The EPA was to develop a national schedule for identifying and cleaning up the nation's worst sites. But payment to private citizens for personal injuries received from toxic chemicals was not provided. Eighteen months past a deadline set by Congress, the EPA in 1982 released a national list of the 418 most hazardous chemical dumps.

By 1989, this list was expanded to nearly 1,200 sites. The EPA has looked at about 28,000 of the nation's 31,000 identified hazardous waste sites, of which about 10,000 have been studied further. Cleanup has begun at over 100 sites. The EPA has recovered more than $2 billion from polluters through legal action.

Cleaning up abandoned waste sites takes time and involves several steps. First, the EPA studies the waste site's characteristics, such as location and type of wastes.

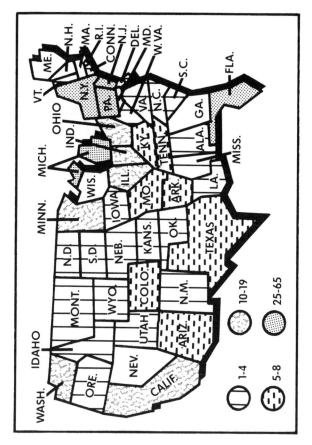

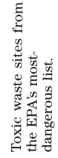

Toxic waste sites from the EPA's most-dangerous list.

The top 20 most hazardous waste sites in the nation.

SITE	CITY OR COUNTY AND STATE
FMC	Fridley, Minnesota
Tybouts Corner	New Castle County, Delaware
Bruin Lagoon	Bruin, Pennsylvania
Industri-Plex	Woburn, Massachusetts
Lipari Landfill	Pitman, New Jersey
Sinclair Refinery	Wellsville, New York
Price Landfill	Pleasantville, New Jersey
Pollution Abatement	Oswego, New York
LaBounty Site	Charles City, Iowa
Helen Kramer Landfill	Mantua, New Jersey
Army Creek	New Castle, Delaware
CPS/Madison Industries	Old Bridge Township, New Jersey
Nyanza Chemical	Ashland, Massachusetts
Gems Landfill	Gloucester Township, New Jersey
Picillo Coventry	Coventry, Rhode Island
Berlin and Farro	Swartz Creek, Michigan
Tar Creek	Cherokee County, Kansas
Baird and McGuire	Holbrook, Massachusetts
Lone Pine Landfill	Freehold, New Jersey
Somersworth Landfill	Somersworth, New Hampshire

Then the agency designs cleanup methods, gets approval for them, and finally carries them out.

Superfund money has been slow in coming, however.

The $1.6 billion in the original Superfund was not enough. The original law expired in September 1985. Cleaning up the nation's abandoned toxic waste dumps is likely to take at least fifty years and cost at least $150 billion, according to a government study.

What did companies think of the old Superfund law? They say it unfairly singled out the chemical and oil industries to pay most cleanup costs. They claim that the toxic-waste problem is everybody's fault, not just the fault of those companies, so we should all help pay for it.

In 1986, a new version of the Superfund law was passed by Congress. The new law provided $8.5 billion over five years, plus $500 million for the cleanup of leaking underground oil storage tanks in thousands of gas stations. Most of this money is coming from taxes on various businesses, not just oil and chemical industries.

The new law sets standards for cleanup and requires work to begin at 375 waste sites. The law encourages the EPA to reach settlements with companies responsible for these sites. The new Superfund will also pay 90 percent of the cost of treating and restoring surface water and groundwater quality.

But even the new law has its critics. These people say that much more money is needed to clean up old, abandoned waste sites. How do we raise hundreds of billions of dollars for this purpose without harming our nation's ability to create jobs and compete with other countries?

To answer this question, let's look at some facts. According to the Superfund law, companies are being held responsible for environmental damage that happened decades earlier. That is true even when those companies acted responsibly.

It is costly and difficult to find out who is responsible for pollution at most older waste sites, because the sites were common dumping areas for several companies. Local, state, and federal governments are spending huge sums to find polluters and fix blame on them.

Cleanup costs are enormous. The average price per waste site is $25 million and can go as high as several billion dollars. So it is not practical for any one company to bear the entire cost. Yet we cannot look to the federal government for help because its budget is already tight.

Thus, our environmental efforts have been slowed down. Most of the action is taking place in court instead of at the waste sites. In some cases, even when insurance companies did not cover pollution damage, the public has turned to them as sources of cleanup funds. But that is no solution. The total cleanup price tag exceeds available funds in all of our insurance companies.

So, how can we fund our national cleanup program? One proposed solution is a National Environmental Trust Fund, controlled by the EPA. This fund would only be used to clean up waste sites. It could be raised by adding a separate fee to business and industrial insurance premiums already being paid.

This new trust fund would only be used for old waste sites. Any future sites would be dealt with on a fault basis, with the polluters paying for the cleanup. The fund would not place too much financial penalty on any one type of business. And, it would avoid much of the time wasted in court trying to fix blame on specific companies. This idea seems to be one that is worth pursuing.

THE TOXIC WASTE GOLDRUSH

Pollution control is one of the fastest growing businesses in America. But until recently, it did not exist because toxic wastes were legally dumped anywhere. The practice of dumping began to change after the Love Canal episode. The Love Canal episode helped to make people aware of toxic dumping. New laws brought the toxic waste industry into being by making it illegal to randomly dump toxic waste.

As a nation, we are trying to find out what to do with the hundreds of millions of tons of toxic waste we produce each year. Burying it has led to problems. Will burning it be any safer?

In 1969, John Rollins came up with the idea of burning hazardous waste in incinerators. He believed that if the waste was burned at high enough temperatures, it would all turn into steam. The amount of heat required to do this would be at least 2000°F.

Since 1969, several hazardous waste incinerators have been built around the country; Rollins owns three of them. Each year, 200 million pounds of hazardous wastes are burned at the Rollins incinerator in Logan Township, New Jersey.

But Rollins has had problems. In 1977, an on-site explosion killed six workers. In 1981, hundreds of thousands of gallons of PCBs and other wastes were spilled. This spill polluted the groundwater in the area.

Rollins answers his critics by saying that industry will always produce toxic waste. And this waste must be treated somewhere. For Rollins, it is a matter of weighing the economic benefits against the risks.

Some experts say that the number of hazardous waste incinerators will increase as landfills run out of space and become fewer in number. But the record of waste disposal companies is troubling. For example, the nation's largest waste disposal company, Waste Management, Inc., was fined $17 million for breaking environmental laws. And Rollins has been fined by state and local governments for the same reason. Yet the industry continues to grow, because of the huge profits that can be made.

So, is the toxic waste cleanup industry part of the solution to our disposal crisis? Or is it part of the problem? Is government doing enough to watch out for the public interest?

Some experts think that cleanup money should not come out of public taxes. It should instead come out of taxes on the industries causing the problem. Then the cost of the goods produced by industries that choose to pollute would contain the cost of cleaning up that waste.

Until Congress makes laws that force companies to reduce their wastes and pretreat them on company property, the public will have to deal with toxic waste disposal sites and incinerators. Until we get to that point, the waste disposal industry will have to dispose of the wastes. And, if government cannot or will not watch over that industry, then the public must do so.

CONCLUSIONS

The controversies over cleanup of hazardous wastes cloud the real issue. Why not use our knowledge of natural cycles (see Chapter 1) to find new ways of recycling these wastes? The surprising fact is that such ways already exist. Without having to come up with brand-new equipment, simple changes in how we use nature and existing equipment would bring about big changes.

For example, a biochemistry professor at Michigan State University has found a common tree fungus that can attack and break down toxic substances. This natural weapon is the white rot fungus, often seen on dead trees. It contains a chemical that biodegrades harmful chemicals into carbon dioxide. It can break down DDT, dioxin, and PCBs, among other substances. This fungus could some day be used to clean up toxic waste sites.

Is it sensible for our government to spend so much time and money tracking new chemical wastes? Is it wise to clean up new and active dump sites but not abandoned ones? The welfare of the people often conflicts with the economic interests of industry, and the government must consider both groups.

AN EXPERIMENT

A Model Chemical-Waste Landfill

Get three large, wide-mouth glass jars of the same size. All should have lids. Label the jars A, B, and C. Use modeling clay to line the sides and bottom of one jar. Use a plastic garbage bag or other piece of plastic to line the second jar. The third jar will not be lined. That is your control. Be sure to wear gloves and safety goggles or glasses while doing this experiment.

Now fill each jar ¾ full with the same kind of soil. Pour equal amounts of the following at a few spots in the soil of each jar: a baking-soda solution; water from a mud puddle; hydrogen peroxide from a supermarket or drugstore; ammonia; alcohol; motor oil; liquid detergent; a liquid fertilizer; and a liquid pesticide or herbicide.

Mark the height of the landfill on the side of each jar with a grease pencil. Cover the jars. Put them in a dark, warm place for two weeks.

Look at the jars at the end of two weeks. Wear gloves and glasses while doing this. Are the contents at the same heights as before? If not, mark their new levels. Remove the lids. Record all observations in your notebook. Carefully and briefly hold each jar and fan the air to smell it. Do not place your nose near any jar. Record how each smells. Do they all smell the same? Then look at the sides and bottom of each jar. Does any jar show leakage of its contents through the linings? Are there any holes in the linings? How wet are the sides and bottom of the control jar compared to the others?

If you wish, cover the jars again. Put them away for another two weeks. What are the levels of the contents after the second two weeks? How much did the contents in each jar sink or leak during the four weeks? What caused them to sink?

A 30-meter high landfill sinks about 1 meter (about 3 feet) in three years. What would happen to houses built on dirt taken from such a landfill? When might such land be safe for building?

Have you figured out the best way to discard the contents of your three models? Consult your science teacher.

CHAPTER 11:
RADIOACTIVE WASTE— FOREVERMORE?

Many toxic waste dumps and landfills are a threat to people's health and well-being. But those threats are mild compared to what will happen if the same mistakes made with toxic wastes are made in handling radioactive waste. As you will see, some mistakes have already been made.

The most serious threat of nuclear waste is not that people will be directly exposed to it but rather that it will get into food chains and water supplies. Radioactive materials give off rays or particles that are absorbed by the cells of living things. Some of this material causes the cells to change and become cancerous. For this and other reasons, today's political decisions and government policies will determine if we have many radioactive Love Canals and Times Beaches in the future.

Let's look at several major types of radioactive waste. We will start with the kind that results from the mining of uranium.

URANIUM MILLS AND MILL TAILINGS

Uranium ore is commonly found in small amounts in certain sedimentary rock. An ore is a rock mixture that contains enough valuable minerals to be mined profitably. This ore is crushed, ground, and dissolved. The uranium is chemically removed. The resulting waste, called *tailings*, is piled near the mill.

For every ton of ore that is processed, 1,996 pounds of tailings are left. They account for 97 percent of the total volume of nuclear wastes, over 3.5 billion cubic feet, according to an article by C. B. Hunt in the *Bulletin of Atomic Scientists*. This huge amount is less radioactive per cubic foot than other nuclear wastes, but there is much more of it. The huge volume of tailings is one reason why they may present the greatest environmental danger of all waste in the future.

Another problem with tailings is that they are left in large piles out in the open. These unfenced piles may emit radiation from radium and thorium contained in the uranium ore. The piles also emit radioactive radon gas and contain toxic heavy metals. Radon is a by-product of the radioactive decay of radium.

Twenty-five million tons of radioactive tailings are stored at eleven sites on the banks of the Colorado River and its tributaries. An estimated 5 million tons of these tailings have blown away or washed into the river. This river system supplies Phoenix, Los Angeles, and much of the Southwest with irrigation and drinking water.

In several western states, where there had been twenty-two uranium mills in the past and where at least sixteen were still operating, the waste material was used as fill for roads and parking lots. It was also used as building material for homes, schools, churches, and businesses. In other words, carcinogens were buried in the homes and workplaces of thousands of people. Today a tailings pile in Durango, Colorado, towers 230 feet above the Animas River.

Most public attention has focused on nuclear power plants as possible threats to us. But the Nuclear Regulatory Commission reports that uranium mining and milling are the most important sources of radiation exposure for the public.

In recent years, Navajo Indians have reported increased levels of lung cancer and birth defects. Many Navajos worked in uranium mines and mills in the 1950s and 1960s. They did not wear protective clothing. They drank water that had seeped down through uranium ore. Lung cancer was unknown in the Navajo community before 1965. Between 1965 and 1979, however, seventeen Navajo men were treated for lung cancer. Sixteen of these patients had mined uranium; fourteen did not smoke.

Cameron, Arizona, saw much uranium mining and milling during the 1950s and 1960s. According to federal health studies, the birth defects rate there is seven times the national average. Families of uranium miners in Red Valley suffer twice as many birth defects, miscarriages, and infant deaths as a group of nonminer families thirty miles away.

All these reports do not prove a link between these medical problems and past uranium development. But they do suggest a possible connection. After all, life and land on the 24,000-square-mile Navajo reservation and across the Southwest have changed a lot since the demand for nuclear weapons and nuclear power began.

Parts of the region had been so extensively mined for coal and uranium that, in 1974, the National Academy of Sciences proposed that these areas be set aside as National Sacrifice Areas. None of the land would be restored to its former beauty. Instead, it would be zoned for mining, intensive energy development would occur there, and no environmental laws or restrictions would apply in such areas. Thus, parts of the Southwest were turned into a domestic energy colony. This occurred after 14 million tons of uranium ore had been taken from 300 mines on the Navajo reservation during the 1950s and 1960s.

Today, Navajo uranium tailings account for 25 percent of the 24 million tons of tailings to be cleaned up. The Nuclear Regulatory Commission estimates that uranium mills will produce seven times the volume of existing tailings by the year 2000.

Navajos believe that the tailings are killing their livestock and that high levels of radiation enter the food chain when cows and sheep graze near and on the edges of tailings piles. Thus, Navajos fear radioactive contamination through their food.

That is not all. Indian children play on tailings piles. They also ride horses on them, even though the radon levels around the piles are ten times the federal standard. This radon is totally unregulated.

In 1978, Congress passed the Uranium Mill Tailings Radiation Control Act. This was supposed to require immediate action by federal and state governments to clean up tailings piles, and prevent the contamination of new areas. The EPA was ordered to develop cleanup and disposal standards for radon emissions from abandoned tailings. The Department of Energy (DOE) was ordered to clean up abandoned piles and handle mill tailings in the future. The Nuclear Regulatory Commission (NRC) was given authority to license the possession of tailings piles at twenty-four abandoned mill sites.

All of these federal agencies were required to act within one year. But none of them did anything to make a difference. They instead avoided the tailings disposal problem. Why? Because the uranium industry by that time was receiving much bad publicity due to public reaction against nuclear power plants. They wanted to keep the problem of tailings hidden.

It took legal action by environmentalists against the EPA, DOE, and NRC for anything to be done. In 1982, the EPA published standards for cleanup of tailings. But these standards are weak. Disposal methods, for example, need to be effective only for 200 years. Radon-gas emissions are not controlled and are acceptable. Tailings need not be buried. And, when it would be very costly to clean up, the uranium industry need not do so.

The EPA estimates that, for every hundred people living near a tailings pile, three will get lung cancer just from exposure to radiation. Ten out of a hundred persons living or working in buildings contaminated with tailings will get lung cancer. These estimates do not include risks of cancers of the liver and spleen. Nor do they include the risks of genetic damage and birth defects.

The mines and mills on the Navajo reservation are quiet now. The nuclear industry's future is being questioned. So the tribe may not have to think about mining and milling of uranium ever again. But tribal leaders say they may consider more uranium development in the National Sacrifice Areas in the future. Meanwhile, across the reservation, community leaders and health workers try to ease the pain of former uranium miners now dying of cancer. And the tailings piles will continue to release radioactivity for another 24,000 years.

WHAT IS RADON?

Radon is a naturally occurring radioactive gas formed as uranium decays in rock and soil. Most radon escapes harmlessly into the air, where it becomes diluted.

Problems occur when radon seeps into houses through cracks and openings in basements. Once indoors, the gas can concentrate and radiation levels rise. Long-term exposure may cause lung cancer because radon decays into tiny solid particles of radioactive polonium. These particles can adhere to airborne dust and smoke, and can be inhaled.

Nearly all the data on the health risks of radon comes from studies of lung cancer rates among uranium miners. In the past, these men were exposed to high levels of the gas. We do not know if the high cancer rates in miners indicate similar risks among people who live in radon-contaminated homes.

Nor do we know how widespread the radon problem is. More than 100,000 homes have been tested. Based on the results, the EPA estimates that at least eight million homes, perhaps as many as 18 million, are contaminated. The EPA plans a national survey, but it won't be finished for several years.

The EPA also estimates that about five million people in Maine, New Hampshire, and Massachusetts may be exposed to radon in water from underground wells. Drinking water high in radon probably is not dangerous. But showering or washing clothes with this water is dangerous, because dissolved radon is released into the indoor air as hot water splashes out of faucets, showers, and washing machines.

According to the EPA, exposure to high radon levels over a long time may account for 5,000 to 20,000 of the 130,000 lung cancer deaths each year in the United States. It is agreed that radon is the main cause of lung cancer in nonsmokers whose homes have had high radon levels for twenty years or more.

Radon detectors are available free or at low cost, from health or environmental agencies. The EPA recommends that measures to reduce radon should be started in any house where tests show high levels of radon.

One measure is to stop all indoor smoking. This will reduce the number of airborne particles that polonium particles can stick to. Ventilation fans can remove radon if levels are not too high.

The most effective solution is to prevent entry of radon by installing plastic pipes over a gravel bed under the basement floor. A small fan attached to the pipes takes out 90 percent of radon-contaminated air from beneath the floor. This air is released outdoors.

Radon can also be removed from well water with a special type of activated carbon filter.

In Sweden, no house can be built until the lot has been tested for radon. If the reading is high, the builder must follow certain building methods to prevent contamination.

Concerned people urge a similar program for all new buildings in the United States, in addition to the use of radon removal systems and radon detectors in existing homes. Testing so far has shown radon areas in nearly every state and in western and eastern Canada.

MILITARY WASTES

Military waste results from the manufacture of nuclear weapons at weapons plants. This waste is stored in about two hundred steel tanks at twenty-one "temporary" sites nationwide. These tanks were built to last more than fifty years. But some began leaking just three years after they were built.

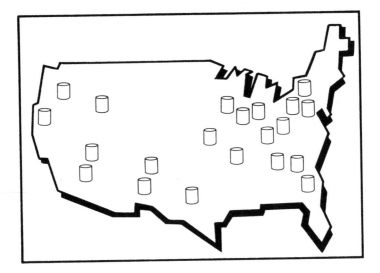

Military wastes are stored in twenty-one sites across the country.

Military waste is much less radioactive than commercial waste. It accounts for only 11 percent of the radioactivity in all American nuclear waste.

How safe are nuclear weapons plants (NWPs)? In 1988, the federal government temporarily closed the Savannah River NWP in Aiken, South Carolina. Officials feared that poor safety practices at the plant would lead to a nuclear accident. Workers at the NWP in Fernald, Ohio, went out on strike in 1988 because their working conditions were too dangerous. Surrounding area residents also claimed that cancerous tumors resulted from the plant's radioactive waste.

Are conditions at U.S. nuclear weapons factories that bad? Many nuclear experts say they are. They want the government to repair, replace, or close down aging NWPs. Other experts agree that the plants need repair, just as many older buildings do. But they claim that most NWPs operate more safely now than they did in the past. These people stress that closing certain plants for long periods could affect our nation's ability to defend itself.

Most radioactive military wastes are stored at the Savannah River plant or the Hanford Reservation plant in Richland, Washington. These plants have stored wastes in underground vaults and aboveground barrels since they opened in the 1950s.

Experts say some of these storage structures have begun to crack, leaking radioactive wastes into the soil. Rainwater that seeps through this soil can carry waste particles into ponds, streams, and well-water supplies.

Some of the leaks may have created health hazards. A government report in 1989 claimed that radioactive materials at the Fernald plant posed a health risk for people nearby. But how much risk is there?

Most doctors believe that brief exposures to very low levels of radioactivity pose little or no risk. Exposure to high levels can cause birth defects, damage the ability to fight off disease, and even start cancerous growths. Yet proving that even long-term exposure to the levels of radioactivity found near NWPs can cause cancer may be difficult.

It costs a lot of money to make old NWPs safe. The Department of Energy decided in 1989 to spend $50 million to remove wastes dumped near one NWP. Experts say that the bill for repairing all U.S. nuclear weapons plants could reach $200 billion over the next twenty years.

Congress would have to approve funds for any cleanup. Some congressional people are not sure whether they are willing to pay. The question is: do we operate a perfect plant? Or do we accept a less-than-perfect plant that is probably safe? That is a hard decision. Is it one that you could make? What should be done with our aging nuclear weapons plants?

COMMERCIAL WASTE

Commercial nuclear waste, including mining wastes, accounts for 89 percent of the radioactivity in American nuclear waste. Such waste consists mostly of used fuel rods stored at nuclear power plants in large pools of water. Commercial waste will keep piling up, even if no new nuclear plants are built. Why? Because waste will keep flowing from the 111 nuclear reactors in operation now, and the 14 others nearing completion. And that waste will continue to be stored "temporarily."

This storage of nuclear waste at power plants is one reason for public concern about nuclear accidents. Two accidents in particular have helped form public opinion: one at Three Mile Island near Harrisburg, Pennsylvania, and the other at the Chernobyl reactor near Kiev in the Soviet Union.

The Three Mile Island accident in March 1979 is considered the worst accident in the history of U.S. commercial nuclear power. One of the two reactors lost its coolant water after a series of mechanical failures and

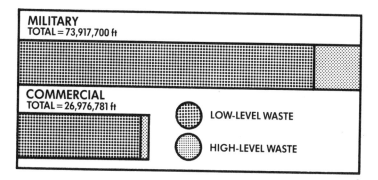

A comparison of the military and commercial sources of radioactive waste.

human errors. The reactor's core became partially uncovered. Small amounts of radiation escaped into the air.

Nobody died as a result of the accident. But the long-term health effects on workers and nearby residents are still being debated. The cleanup of the damaged reactor will probably cost $1 billion to $1.5 billion. The electric utility that owns the plant gave out confusing statements about the seriousness of the accident. So did the NRC. Such statements created fears about the safety of nuclear power.

The world's worst nuclear disaster occurred in April 1986. Two gas explosions occurred inside one of four water-cooled nuclear reactors at Chernobyl, blowing the roof off the reactor building. The graphite core of the reactor was set on fire. The accident occurred when engineers had turned off most of the reactor's safety and warning systems in order to conduct a safety experiment.

The explosions and fire spewed highly radioactive materials into the air. These were carried by winds over parts of the Soviet Union and much of Europe. Hazardous radioactive matter fell more than 1,250 miles from the plant in over twenty countries. Firefighters took ten days to get the hot graphite fire under control. During those ten days, 135,000 people living within eighteen miles of the site were carried out by 1,100 buses. These people have been resettled in other villages. They will not be allowed to return to their homes for at least several years.

Five months after the accident, thirty-one plant workers and firefighters died from exposure to high radiation levels. Two hundred others suffered from radiation sickness. One thousand square miles of surrounding land were contaminated. All nearby forests were cut down. The topsoil was removed and buried. Farmland in the area will remain abandoned.

Medical experts estimate that perhaps 100,000 people in the Soviet Union will die prematurely over the next seventy years from radiation-caused cancer. Thousands of others will have eye cataracts and be sterile. Three times as many premature deaths are likely outside the Soviet Union.

Estimated damages run from $3 billion to $5 billion. But long-term health effects will raise this figure to nearly $14 billion.

No commercial nuclear reactors have been ordered in the United States since 1978. Since Three Mile Island and Chernobyl, the future for nuclear energy may seem even bleaker. Some experts believe that nuclear power is our best option for producing electricity—but only if it can be made safer.

LOW-LEVEL WASTES

Most military and commercial wastes are low level. This includes mildly contaminated laboratory equipment. It is harmless after a few weeks or months. It includes slightly contaminated clothing, paper, solutions used in medicine, plastics, and tools. But it also includes sludge from reactors. This sludge remains hazardous for several hundred years, depending on the material it's in.

All radioactive elements change to other elements as a result of the radiation. Their nuclei change to other elements, some of which are not radioactive. Each radioactive element decays at a different speed. The *half-life* of a radioactive substance is the time it takes for half the amount in a sample to decompose. The half-life of radium is 1,620 years; for uranium it is 5 billion years; and for thorium it is 1,390 billion years. The half-life of the radioactive chemicals used in hospitals is minutes or hours.

How do we dispose of all this waste? Since the 1960s, most low-level waste has been buried shallowly at six commercial dumps. At one, near Sheffield, Illinois, burial trenches holding nearly 3.1 million cubic feet of low-level waste have been collapsing. Opened in 1967, Sheffield closed in 1978 after buried radioactive tritium (a radioactive form of hydrogen) showed up in nearby test wells.

Two other dumps, in Kentucky and New York, were likewise closed by 1978 after radioactive materials seeped out of their trenches.

This shutdown of half the nation's low-level dumps occurred during an increase in the amount of waste being produced. So there was much concern over where to put it. Congress decided the problem was one for the states.

THE LOW-LEVEL RADIOACTIVE WASTE POLICY ACT

In 1980, Congress passed an act that affected radioactive waste. This act holds every state responsible for the low-level waste it produces. A state may set up its own dump, or it may form a compact with other nearby states and create a regional dump. It must do one or the other by 1993. Once a regional compact is formed, its members may decide to keep out the waste from other states. So far, six compacts have been formed. But until 1993, all fifty states are allowed to continue dumping at three sites in Nevada, Washington, and South Carolina.

More important is another effect of the 1980 act. It guarantees that the mistakes of the past will be repeated. It does this by forcing the establishment of poorly designed waste-burial grounds in unsuitable regions, such as the humid and heavily populated Northeast. In ordering the regional compacts, Congress took no account of the wide variations in population and yearly rainfall among the different regions. It also ignored the huge risks in shallow land burial of nuclear waste in wet climates.

All three closings of waste dumps by 1978 occurred in wet, humid climates.

Increasingly fearful of being a regional dump state, many states are considering their own burial sites. But this was not the purpose of the act. It wanted only several dumps, not fifty. Yet environmental groups would rather have fifty dumps. A dump in each state would cut down on the transport of waste between states, and the waste would be better controlled.

NUCLEAR WEAPONS WASTE

Meanwhile, the world's first permanent storehouse for low-level nuclear waste from weapons plants is being built. It is the Waste Isolation Pilot Plant (WIPP), a maze of tunnels carved from salt beds 2,150 feet underground, twenty-six miles east of Carlsbad, New Mexico.

In 1988, DOE engineers questioned the safety of this $680-million dump site. Water was entering through cracks in the walls. Some scientists believe that these leaks could make the site unfit for permanently storing one million barrels of low-level nuclear wastes. The barrels contain cast-off gloves, tools, clothing, leftover bomb materials, plutonium-tainted equipment, toxic chemicals, heavy metals, and decomposing organic matter. These materials have half-lives measured in thousands of years.

The barrels will be placed in the chambers after crossing more than twenty states. When the caverns are filled, the shafts will be plugged and the site abandoned. If leaks are found after five years, the DOE says it will recover the 125,000 barrels of waste that are expected to be buried by that time.

But leaks have already been found. Some experts think that moisture in the chambers might mix with salt. This could form 250,000 gallons of corrosive salt water. It could eat through the steel drums, releasing radioactivity into the Pecos River, a tributary of the Rio Grande.

DOE officials, however, think that these concerns are blown out of proportion. They say that the existing method of "temporarily" storing plutonium wastes in shallow trenches at various places is far more hazardous. They claim that, at most, about 10,000 gallons of salt water would flow into a storage chamber.

There are other safety concerns. The type of container used to transport waste to the dump site has often failed its impact tests. Little money is available to train and equip emergency teams along shipping routes. And the EPA has not approved burial of mixed radioactive and toxic wastes at the site.

The DOE has searched for a safe method of radioactive waste disposal since the 1950s. And it has handled nuclear waste poorly at nearly all of its weapons plants. Indeed, the DOE needs the Carlsbad dump site to improve its public image as well as to help clean up and modernize its aging weapons plants.

HIGH-LEVEL WASTE

The U.S. government has also not done well in providing long-term storage of high-level waste. Such waste includes used fuel rods from nuclear power plants. This material remains deadly for 10,000 years.

Originally, fuel rods were to be stored "temporarily" at the nuclear power plants. After several years, they were to be shipped to government storage areas. The government promised by that time the storage depots would be ready.

But the government has not kept its promise. So some companies have transferred their excess fuel rods from one nuclear power plant to another. Clearly, something has to be done. After all, this is the nation's most complex and possibly deadly industrial-waste problem.

High-level liquid wastes from nuclear weapons production also await permanent storage. These wastes stay deadly for centuries. They are currently stored in underground tanks at government plants in Idaho, South Carolina, and Washington.

These tanks must be watched for leaks. Nearly 550,000 gallons of highly radioactive wastes have already leaked from older tanks.

After thirty years of research, there is still no scientific solution to the problem of safely storing high-level wastes for the 10,000 years required by the EPA. Most citizens oppose placing a burial site near their homes.

THE NUCLEAR WASTE POLICY ACT

In 1982, Congress passed the Nuclear Waste Policy Act. This set a schedule for the DOE to choose a site and build the nation's first deep underground burial place for permanent storage of high-level waste.

This waste consists of spent fuel from commercial nuclear reactors. Also included are solid by-products from the manufacture of nuclear explosives. These by-products contain highly toxic plutonium, with a half-life of 24,000 years. More than 20,000 tons of this waste have built up over the years. The amount increases by 2,000 tons each year.

By 1985, the DOE had narrowed the search for suitable burial sites to three places. One was a salt deposit in Deaf Smith County, Texas. Another was in a volcanic basalt formation under the Hanford, Washington, nuclear weapons plant. The third was in a volcanic ash formation in Yucca Mountain, Nevada, 115 miles northwest of Las Vegas. The DOE tests nuclear weapons underground near this last site.

Each site was to be studied for five years. Then the President would decide, in 1991, which site would be used. The first burial place would fill up quickly with wastes already awaiting storage. Thus, a second site was to be found in the eastern United States, where most reactors are located.

However, by 1986, there was intense opposition from citizens and elected officials. For one thing, geologists found geological and underground water problems with each site. Secondly, if the waste were transported to the sites by truck, 6,000 shipments each year would pass through forty-five states. If the waste traveled by rail, there would be 830 shipments each year. A study by the NRC concluded that a serious accident involving a truck or train could result in $3 billion worth of damages.

In 1987, Congress eliminated the Texas and Washington sites, partly as a result of political pressure from those states. Yucca Mountain was picked as the only site for further study.

The EPA requires that the waste, whenever it is buried, be prevented from contaminating the surrounding area for 10,000 years. Engineers must also consider that American society might not survive the next few hundred years. Nuclear war or some other catastrophe could cause this waste to be exposed. If the DOE decides that Yucca Mountain is suitable, workers could start building 1,500 acres of tunnels deep inside the mountain by 1998. Five years later, the burial of waste-filled canisters will start. Each canister will weigh 100 tons and be surrounded by steel and concrete. About fifty years from now, the site will be filled with some 70,000 tons of waste.

The canisters are expected to contain the waste for up to 1,000 years. Then Yucca Mountain itself must do the job. The mountain seems able to do this. It is made of volcanic ash that long ago hardened into rock.

Other advantages of this site include its remoteness. It is a dozen miles from the nearest settlement. It is also dry, with only six inches of rainfall a year. The water table is 2,500 feet below the surface. The burial place would be built about 1,000 feet above this water table.

Still, some people are worried about this site. A few minor but active geological faults dot the region. A cinder cone fifteen miles south of Yucca Mountain has erupted often during the ten-million-year history of the area. Another eruption within several thousand years could indirectly damage the burial site by changing groundwater flow patterns.

Other experts claim that a century of storing waste at reactor sites would be safer than burying it in southern Nevada, because geologic conditions at Yucca Mountain are poorly understood. They also say that the amount of radioactivity in high-level waste dies down after several decades.

These people would like to delay permanent storage of the waste. This would allow radiation in old commercial reactors to decrease and they would then be simpler to take apart. But utility companies don't want to spend large amounts of money to guard nuclear waste for 100 years. However, a delay would also buy time to further our knowledge of the geology of the Nevada site, as well as possible future climate changes.

The DOE continues to study Yucca Mountain so that the first canisters of waste can be buried by 2003. But delays in such schedules are common. The first burial site was supposed to be ready by 1998. But in 1987 the DOE postponed that to at least 2003, and most people believe it will be further delayed to 2008.

Meanwhile, several utility companies have begun building giant tanks to store their spent nuclear fuel. This action became necessary as the pools inside their reactor buildings filled up with high-level nuclear waste.

CONCLUSIONS

The commercial nuclear industry began in the 1950s. At that time, government, business, and science all promised a solution to the problem of radioactive waste. As we have seen, however, a workable solution has not been found.

The burden remains on the public to prove the nuclear industry is hazardous; no one seems to expect the industry to prove it is truly safe. Unless this changes, not many years will pass before radioactive waste joins with toxic chemicals in a massive destruction of our lives and health.

AN EXPERIMENT

Model Tailings Piles

Make two piles of sand, one wet and one dry. Be sure they are the same size. Use a fan to simulate wind at an equal distance from each pile. Which pile's sand grains blow away faster?

Then sprinkle a bucket of water on each pile. Do not pour it heavily. Which pile cracks faster? What do these demonstrations tell you about the effects of humid and dry climates on the erosion of tailings piles?

CHAPTER 12:
WHAT PRICE CLEAN AIR?

Thus far we have discussed problems of burying waste underground. Let's now consider problems of disposing of it in the air.

INDUSTRIAL SMOG

Coal and oil contain small amounts (0.5 to 5 percent) of sulfur. When the coal is burned, the sulfur reacts with oxygen to form a gas, sulfur dioxide (SO_2). Within several days, most of this gas is changed to sulfur trioxide (SO_3), which reacts with water in the air to form droplets of sulfuric acid (H_2SO_4). This mist eats away metals and other materials. It can irritate and damage the lungs. Tiny particles of sulfuric acid released from coal and oil combustion and dust in the air give mist a gray color. Then it is known as *smog*. The word *smog* is a contraction of the words smoke and fog.

In many regions, this mist is washed out of the atmosphere by rain or blown away by wind within several days. However, if there is no rain or wind, these particles of sulfuric acid, which absorb all kinds of chemicals, can build up to deadly levels, especially in industrial cities. The smaller the particle, the more easily it can penetrate all the way into the lungs. But the larger particles are trapped in the nasal passage, coughed up, or perhaps swallowed. Buildups of chemical particles caused air pollution disasters in London in 1952 (4,000 deaths) and 1956 (900 deaths). Other disasters occurred in Donora, Pennsylvania, in 1948 (20 deaths, 6,000 sick) and in New York City in 1965 (400 deaths).

PHOTOCHEMICAL SMOG

Another type of smog, photochemical smog, occurs in nonindustrial cities with warm, dry climates. In such places, cars and trucks are the main sources of air contaminants. Nitrogen and oxygen do not combine at normal temperatures. But they do react at the high temperatures inside an engine. They produce nitric oxide (NO). This gas comes out in car exhaust. It combines with oxygen in the atmosphere to form nitrogen dioxide (NO_2), a reddish brown gas that causes a brownish smog, and other nitrogen- and oxygen-containing gases often referred to as NO_x.

Most air pollution problems with NO and NO_2 arise when ultraviolet radiation from sunlight causes them to combine with car and truck hydrocarbons, and with the oxygen in the air, to form photochemical smog. This smog can cause the eyes to smart, damage crops, corrode paint, buildings, and statues, and rot nylon and leather. It causes headaches, bronchitis, or lung diseases, depending on the kinds of chemicals adsorbed on the small particles.

Yet the air pollution picture is not totally bleak. In 1986, scientists discovered a chemical process capable of removing nitrogen oxides from diesel exhaust and smoke from coal-fired boilers. The hot gases, passed over a nontoxic chemical, break down into harmless nitrogen and water.

CARBON DIOXIDE AND THE GREENHOUSE EFFECT

Carbon dioxide is building up in the atmosphere, largely because of the burning of fossil fuels. And there are several other gases that have an even greater ability to trap heat. These gases include methane, nitrous oxides, and chlorofluorocarbons. Nearly all of these gases come from human-made sources such as vehicle exhausts and industrial chemicals. Only a small amount comes from natural sources like soil bacteria.

In the atmosphere, these gases act like the glass in a greenhouse. They let in sunlight but trap heat. They do this by absorbing rather than reflecting the infrared radiation that produces heat. Thus, they cause a warming of the planet called the "greenhouse effect." The gases are called "greenhouse gases."

Scientists predict several results of the greenhouse effect. World temperatures are expected to rise between 2°F and 8°F by the middle of the next century, if not sooner. Temperature increases would be greater near the Arctic and Antarctic, and smaller near the Equator. Wind and rainfall patterns would change. This would mean that some farming areas, such as the midwestern United States, would have shorter growing seasons. Other farming areas, such as the Soviet Union, would have longer seasons. Sea levels would rise, flooding major cities along our coasts. Droughts would get worse. Hurricanes and other storms would be more violent.

Rapid cutting and burning of forests pumps more carbon dioxide into the atmosphere, speeding up the warming of the planet. Nowhere is this occurring more rapidly than in the rain forest of Central America and northern South America. This forest covered 400,000 square miles just 100 years ago. It now covers only a few thousand square miles, and is being cut and burned at the rate of 30 to 50 acres a minute during the dry season (May through October).

Why is this forest being cut? For one thing, the mineral wealth beneath it is enormous. Iron ore, copper, gold, tin, and other ores could make Brazil and other developing nations in this area very prosperous.

Also, the governments of such countries have given tax breaks and loans to settlers who will cut the trees and farm the land as well as raise cattle for export. In fact, much of the meat from these cattle has found its way to the United States as fast-food hamburgers, pet foods, baby foods, luncheon meats, and frozen dinners. And in many parts of Brazil, Peru, Ecuador, and Colombia, farmers raise coca plants in the cut areas, according to the Sierra Club. The narcotic drug cocaine is made from these coca plants.

Brazilians cannot understand why North Americans and Europeans want them to stop cutting the rain forest. After all, we cut our forests when we settled and farmed our land. But there are several reasons why the Amazon forest is so valuable.

For one thing, this forest is believed to house millions of plant and animal species, many of them yet to be identified. But we know that almost all prescription drugs have been made from tropical plants. Why destroy something that may have great medical value?

Another reason for not cutting this forest is that its soil is thin and poor. Those people who burn trees exhaust the soil after several years of farming and ranching.

The rain forest releases and absorbs much moisture. As the forest disappears, the Amazon basin may be wiped out with floods during the wet season. The bare clay in cut areas will become desert in the dry season.

In addition, Brazil's treatment of the forest is total destruction, not controlled development. In 1987, for example, 170,000 fires were started in the western Amazon alone as settlers cut and burned the land. A total of 6,000 fires were started in one day! Only 5 percent of the cut trees are sold for lumber. The rest are burned or left to decay, adding more carbon dioxide to the atmosphere.

Meanwhile, thousands of gold miners in the forest are leaching ore with mercury, a fearful poison. They dump 40 tons of this mercury a year into the rivers. Mercury biomagnifies through food chains. How long will it take to make its way into the human diet?

Lastly, the chemical companies that make pesticides which are banned in the United States send 40 percent of them to Brazil, helping that nation's cut-and-burn farming and ranching operations.

In 1989, Brazil's president suspended the tax breaks and loans to farmers and ranchers for ninety days. He said cattle-ranching would be limited in the Amazon. The construction of government roads, dams, and mines in the rain forest was also suspended. He started a five-year, $100 million program to zone the Amazon for farming and mining. He began to control the production and sale of toxic chemicals used there. The Brazilian president also created seven million acres of national parks. All of this will cost $350 million during the first two years.

The president tried to stop exports of wood from Brazil. But, today, these exports go on. The cutting and burning go on. Meanwhile, the world's climate continues to change. And the global carbon cycle becomes disrupted still more as the Amazon spews 7 percent of the world's carbon dioxide into the air.

CARBON MONOXIDE

When hydrocarbons or carbon in coal are not completely burned, carbon monoxide (CO) results. It is a colorless and odorless gas that surrounds cities in con-

Two "classic" with and without photos of Los Angeles smog.

Photos courtesy South Coast Air Quality Management District

centrations greater than those of any other toxic chemical in air.

The greatest source of CO in the air around cities is the motor vehicle. Inhaled carbon monoxide reacts with the blood, taking the place of its oxygen, thus preventing oxygen transport. This can lead to headaches, fatigue, heart disease, and with heavy exposure to death. In terms of the total amount of each contaminant in air, carbon monoxide ranks highest, making the car the major source of air pollution.

But let's consider how harmful each chemical is. On this basis, sulfur oxides and tiny particles rank highest. Coal-burning power plants are the most hazardous air pollution sources on this basis. Industries come in second, while cars and trucks are third.

OZONE

Ozone at ground level is a pollutant. It is formed by complex chemical reactions that mix organic compounds with nitrogen oxides in the presence of heat and sunlight. Therefore, ozone pollution occurs mainly during the warmer months.

Ground-level ozone differs from high-atmosphere ozone. The high-atmosphere ozone occurs naturally. Found between 10 and 30 miles up, it shields the planet from the sun's ultraviolet rays. Ozone molecules each consist of three oxygen atoms. These absorb most of the ultraviolet rays that are otherwise dangerous to life on earth.

Scientists are concerned that the high-atmosphere

ozone is being depleted by chlorofluorocarbons (CFCs). When they were first made in the 1930s, CFCs seemed too good to be true. Consisting of chlorine, fluorine, and carbon, CFCs are nontoxic and do not combine easily with other substances. Because they vaporize at low temperatures, they are perfect as coolants in refrigerators and air conditioners. They are also used as propellants in spray cans. They are good insulators and are therefore standard ingredients in plastic foam materials like Styrofoam. CFCs are also cheap and simple to make.

Spray cans, discarded or leaking refrigerators and air conditioners, and the burning of plastic foam items all release CFCs. Over several decades, they gradually move higher into the atmosphere. As they get hit with ultraviolet rays, they break down, releasing chlorine atoms that speed up the breakdown of ozone into oxygen.

Why is the breakdown of ozone so dangerous? Besides causing sunburn, ultraviolet rays have been linked to skin cancer, eye problems, and weakened ability of humans and animals to fight off infection.

In the 1970s scientists first warned that CFCs could attack ozone in the upper atmosphere. The United States, Canada, and most Scandinavian countries banned the use of CFCs in spray cans in 1978. But the rest of the world kept using CFC-based spray cans. Overall CFC production grew.

The threat became clearer in 1985, when scientists reported a "hole" in the ozone layer over Antarctica. The extent of this hole varies with the seasons and weather. A smaller hole has also been discovered over the Arctic.

As a result of these discoveries, fifty-three nations met

in 1987 and agreed to cut back on the use of CFCs by 50 percent by 1999. These nations included the United States and the Soviet Union.

But that is not good enough. The same stability that makes CFCs so safe for industrial use makes them persistent in the upper atmosphere. When plastic foam hamburger packages are broken, CFCs escape. They also escape from discarded refrigerators and when auto air conditioners are drained.

The only sure way to save the ozone layer is a complete ban on CFC production. But a ban would disturb the worldwide $2.2 billion annual market for CFCs. So, most nations are phasing out their CFCs over five years.

To make this phase-out easier, chemical companies are trying to find substitutes for CFCs. But substitutes will cost much more to make. This higher cost will be passed on to the public. But the only other choice is to allow the life-saving ozone layer to be destroyed.

LEAD

Certain chemicals added to gasoline can cause additional hazardous wastes in car exhausts. One of these substances is tetraethyl lead, which makes car engines run more smoothly by preventing the engine from knocking. Everyone is exposed to tetraethyl lead in air, drinking water, and food. In our nation, 90 percent of the 120 million pounds of airborne lead each year comes from leaded gasoline in cars. Another 5 percent comes from industrial smelters. We get small amounts of lead from the

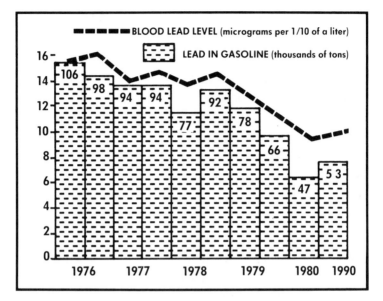

Lead in gasoline and blood lead levels.

air, our food, and our water. A 1986 EPA study showed that 77 percent of the U.S. population have unsafe lead levels in their blood. This includes 88 percent of children under age five.

An estimated 300,000 American children, especially those in low-income families, are exposed to high lead levels from still another source. These children peel off paint chips from walls. Old paint contains lead compounds. The children eat the chips and are often severely poisoned by the lead in the paint. About 200 die each year; another 12,000 to 16,000 are treated for lead poisoning. They have palsy, partial paralysis, or even permanent brain damage. Paint containing lead compounds cannot be purchased today.

Lead biomagnifies. Thus, the more that is inhaled or eaten, the more it builds up in the blood. Luckily, most lead is expelled in the urine fast enough to keep the blood lead level low. But this does not happen in cases of continued exposure at high concentrations.

Many scientists have urged that lead additives be banned from gasoline. They also urge smelters and other industries to control their release of lead. National studies also show a link between lead levels in gasoline and the average lead level in the blood of the American population.

Using unleaded gasoline pays off in three ways. It keeps lead from poisoning the air. It reduces car care. And it allows a catalytic converter to do its job.

Converters have been on new cars sold in America since 1975. Converters remove 90 percent of carbon monoxide and hydrocarbons from gasoline. They also reduce nitrogen oxides. But only a few tankfuls of leaded gas can destroy the converter's effectiveness.

Due in large part to unleaded gas and catalytic converters, the levels of lead, carbon monoxide, and sulfur dioxide in the air have declined somewhat since 1978. But they must be reduced still more.

In 1984, the EPA announced a proposal to reduce the lead content of gasoline from 1.1 grams per gallon to 0.1 gram, starting in 1986. The oil and lead industries said this would increase the cost of gasoline. It would also require more foreign oil to be imported because larger amounts of crude oil are needed to produce unleaded fuel with power equal to that of leaded fuel.

The EPA, however, said the number of imported barrels would rise by only several thousand. It also claimed the oil industry would have to pay $575 million to cover higher refining costs. This cost would raise the price of gasoline about two cents per gallon.

Meanwhile, the leading American producer of tetraethyl lead additives for gasoline, Ethyl Corporation, vowed to fight any more rules on leaded fuel. It believes any further reduction of lead is unnecessary. It said the EPA should consider other causes of lead deposits in human blood, including the eating of leaded paint by children. Today, new cars are manufactured to use only unleaded gasoline.

CONTROLLING AUTO POLLUTION

Control of toxic chemicals in vehicle exhausts is important, but difficult. It is harder to control toxic chemicals from 190 million moving cars and 45 million trucks than from several thousand nonmoving industrial sources.

In 1965, Congress passed the Motor Vehicle Air Pollution Control Act. It established national standards for auto exhausts, to be effective in 1968. But by 1970, American car makers had still not developed a completely clean engine.

Different fuels could reduce auto pollutants. Two fuels being studied are compressed natural gas and methanol. Both produce cleaner exhaust gases than either gasoline or diesel fuel. Alcohol fuels, such as methanol and ethanol, are seen as good fuels for smog-ridden cities. Methanol exhaust gases produce only 20 to 33 percent of the low-level ozone that would be made by an equal amount of current fuel.

Methanol is made with 85 percent natural gas and 15 percent unleaded gas. It can also be made with coal. And the United States has lots of coal. Methanol also has the potential to lower the levels of carbon monoxide in the air.

But methanol has disadvantages. Cars must have larger gas tanks to carry it. As it burns, methanol releases cancer-causing formaldehyde, which must be removed by a catalytic converter. Methanol also gives off carbon dioxide. This gas is a major culprit behind the greenhouse effect.

The methanol issue is caught in a trap. Oil companies won't produce it in great amounts until enough methanol-fueled cars are on the road. Auto makers won't make methanol-fueled cars until the oil companies produce more methanol. Auto makers also believe that new fuels will never replace current ones until worldwide oil prices increase many times.

What about electric cars? Some have been on the road for years. But such cars need large batteries and the batteries take all night to recharge.

Thus, our energy future is as uncertain as the future of the personal car. We don't have a sound national energy policy, partly because our energy problem is part of a global energy shortage. We must therefore try to find global solutions to the energy problem if we want a decent energy future—indeed, if we want any future at all.

AIR QUALITY LAWS

A public outcry over industrial smog in the 1950s and early 1960s led Congress to pass the Clean Air Act in 1965 and the Air Quality Act in 1967. These were the first federal environmental laws. They stated that the government was responsible for protecting people against unhealthy air. Scientists were asked to find out how clean the air should be.

But it soon became clear these laws were not working. Why? There was as yet no EPA or any other enforcement agency. The EPA did not exist until 1970. Furthermore, industry fought the clean air laws.

Now public pressure became stronger and was applied to the auto industry as well as to Congress. In response, Congress passed the 1970 Clean Air Act changes, or amendments. This law required new industries, power plants, and cars to limit their pollution.

Realizing each state has different air problems, the law gave states the job of putting plans together to reach the federal standards. A state could have more stringent standards but at least had to meet the federal standards. Industries in each state were to use the best available methods to clean up. They were also to search for better methods. Otherwise, the federal government would step in.

The law gave industry a deadline. A timetable was set up, aimed at reducing hydrocarbons from new cars by 90 percent in five years. Similar deadlines were set for other industries.

All these deadlines were not met for two reasons. First, between 1970 and 1974, American auto makers continued their slow progress in controlling hydrocarbons. Second, Iran stopped sending oil to America and western Europe in 1973. Americans thus had an oil shortage. Since pollution-control devices require more fuel, research into reducing auto hydrocarbons ceased.

During all this time, car companies and other industries tried to get Congress to weaken the Clean Air Act. Environmental groups wanted it strengthened to prevent further delays. In 1977, Congress weakened its 1970 act.

Congress postponed deadlines that were set by the 1970 act. The nation was given until 1982 to meet the minimum air quality standards for tiny particles, hydrocarbons, carbon monoxide, sulfur dioxide, and lead. It was given until 1987 to meet the standards for nitrogen oxides. In 1985, the deadline was postponed again, to 1988.

Under the existing law, cities were required to reduce ground-level ozone and carbon monoxide enough to meet the federal air-quality standards by December 31, 1987. If this deadline was not met, the EPA could cut off funds for construction of highways and sewage-treatment plants near cities.

The deadline continues to be postponed because nearly 100 cities have not met the federal standards. Meanwhile, scientists have found at least 600 potentially hazardous pollutants in air.

EFFECTS OF THE CLEAN AIR ACT

Has the Clean Air Act worked? Many industries complain about it. They say its strict standards make it cheaper to build new plants in other countries, which weakens the American economy. They also say the high cost of placing pollution controls in existing factories makes it cheaper just to close them. But it is almost impossible for them to find locations for new plants. In some areas, federal law does not allow existing good quality air to be polluted. Plants cannot be located in other areas because the air is already dirty.

Environmental groups say the health benefits from air control far outweigh the costs. The money spent on control has not slowed overall economic growth. It has increased such growth by making more jobs in the pollution-control industry. Pollution control only slightly increases prices. Plant closings blamed on control standards have been few. Present standards should not slow down the development of any American energy resource.

Environmental groups, however, complain that the EPA has set standards for only eight airborne chemicals. It has set no standards at all for carbon tetrachloride, chloroform, formaldehyde, and other pollutants. Standards have been set for mercury, vinyl chloride, asbestos, arsenic, beryllium, benzene, sulfuric acid, and radioactive substances.

Why have standards been set for only eight air pollutants? In part, because whenever the EPA proposes an emission standard, industry sues the agency. One possible solution: change the act to require installation of all technology available to control all toxic emissions rather than trying to control one chemical at a time.

The EPA, meanwhile, wants any new Clean Air Act to allow an industry-by-industry approach to the air pollution problem. How would this work?

First, the EPA would rank industries according to the amount of toxic chemicals they produce. The chemical industry, petroleum refining, and the manufacturing of tires would be high on this list.

Then, the EPA would judge the cost of cleanup methods that are available to each industry. The agency would order various toxic-producing companies to use those cleanup methods. Refineries, for instance, might be told to light flares on their smokestacks to burn off organic chemicals. Other industries might have to install filters on smokestacks to trap metal particles.

The future of the nation, in fact, is starting to look much like California. In 1989, Los Angeles air-quality officials proposed a strong, three-level anti-pollution plan.

Level I, required by 1993, does not call for any new technology. It outlaws new drive-through features in fast-food places. This keeps cars from idling in lines. Level I also promotes van-pooling. It charges families a premium to own more than one car.

Level II would be in place by the year 2000. It requires much cleanup of electric-power plants and oil refineries in the Los Angeles area.

Level III is scheduled for the year 2007. It requires the development of brand-new technology, such as electric cars.

Whether the rest of our nation will copy California's plan is anyone's guess. It is hoped that a new Clean Air Act will not have to wait for an air pollution emergency. A new act is sensible, and long overdue.

In 1989, President Bush asked that the act be changed. According to his plan, sulfur dioxide emissions from coal-burning power plants would be cut by ten million tons by the year 2000. Emissions of nitrogen oxides would be cut by two million tons a year, or one-tenth their present rate. Half of these cuts must be done by 1995 and the rest by 2000. Companies would be free to decide how to reach these goals. They could use scrubbers (devices on smokestacks that remove sulfur chemically). Companies could burn low-sulfur coal. They could encourage their customers to conserve electricity, which would reduce the amount of coal burned. Or, companies could invent new technology that allows them to burn coal without producing polluting gases. Companies that choose new technology would have until 2003 to meet the final deadline.

The first phase of required cuts would affect over 100 power plants in eighteen states. Plants in the same state would be allowed to trade pollution rights. This means that if a company were to exceed the required cuts, it could sell the rights to release extra pollution to other companies. They could also transfer these rights to other plants within the same company.

The President's plan also required all but a few of the nearly 100 cities with ozone problems to reach an ozone standard level by the year 2000. Los Angeles, New York, and Houston would be given until 2010 to reach the standard. But these cities would have to file annual progress reports.

President Bush's plan called for the use of cleaner-burning fuels like natural gas and alcohol instead of gasoline. The plan would also force auto makers and oil companies to speed up the pace of producing different fuels and vehicles that use them. One Bush proposal called for methanol-fueled cars in nine heavily polluted cities by 1995, and a million more such cars being produced each year after 1997. The auto industry claimed that this was not enough time.

The President's plan required the twenty cities with the worst ozone problems to cut such pollution by 3 percent a year. Cities with carbon monoxide problems would use fuel that produces less carbon monoxide. Denver, Colorado, is already doing this with gasoline that has extra oxygen added.

The President also told the EPA to set up a plan that would allow car makers to reach anti-pollution deadlines by trading pollution rights, just like power companies.

Critics of the plan said that the pollution trading policy could be easily abused. They said that the cuts in ozone, carbon monoxide, nitrogen oxides, and sulfur dioxide levels were not enough. The oil and electric utility companies said that certain requirements in the President's plan were too much.

The President's proposals could require payments of up to $18 billion a year by these industries. They claimed that this would be too heavy a burden, because each year they already spend over $30 billion on pollution-control equipment.

Critics of the plan likewise fear that the entire American economy would be burdened. They fear higher electricity prices for the public and for industry, which would, in turn, raise the prices of many manufactured goods. Industries also fear that the costs of cleaning up the air could slow down their ability to compete in world markets.

But President Bush's proposals could lower present costs to public health and the environment caused by air pollution. The American Lung Association estimates these costs to be $16 billion to $40 billion each year.

The plan could force some companies to use more modern equipment, making them more efficient in the long run. Companies that make pollution-control equipment would also benefit. So would the public. These proposals would be costly. Yet national polls show that people are generally willing to pay their fair share of this cost, as long as they know that industry is cooperating.

FORMALDEHYDE

Between 1981 and 1984, more than two thousand lawsuits over exposure to formaldehyde were filed in the United States. They charge that formaldehyde exposure has resulted in infant deaths, adult brain damage, and other health tragedies.

Formaldehyde causes other problems, too. One of these is "sensitivity." The body becomes sensitized to many substances made from formaldehyde; rashes, headaches, nausea, and breathing problems result.

Formaldehyde is present in certain chemicals, drugs, and cosmetics. Over 7 billion pounds of formaldehyde are made annually. It was also used in a plastic foam that was injected into the paneling and insulation of many walls, especially in mobile homes. In fact, people with the greatest risk are those living in trailers. People are also at risk in other homes with new foam insulation, plywood, or paneling. The better sealed a home or trailer is, the higher the levels of formaldehyde.

Formaldehyde is a carcinogen in rats at high levels. It causes changes in the linings of air passages in monkeys. These changes are thought to be the early stages of cancer. Formaldehyde also causes mutations in bacteria. So far, there is little evidence linking formaldehyde to human cancer.

The U.S. Consumer Product Safety Commission banned formaldehyde foam insulation in 1981, but this ban was removed in 1983. The EPA has the power to regulate formaldehyde under the Toxic Substances Control Act. Yet the EPA has not done so, because it says that no studies prove that formaldehyde is carcinogenic in people.

But many scientists say that the EPA should ban formaldehyde in plywood and paneling. They also believe that states should require local building codes to require more ventilation in homes. Such codes would limit the exposure to all indoor air pollutants.

But those codes are not set up for two reasons. First, climate control systems are often desired in buildings to keep a constant temperature during the year. Such systems demand airtight buildings. Second, many people try to conserve energy in homes. They do this by installing insulation to seal leaks and cracks.

A balance is therefore needed between achieving

energy conservation and providing ventilation. Japan, Sweden, and West Germany have ventilation codes. They also conserve energy. We can and must do the same.

ASBESTOS

Asbestos is a natural mineral that resists fire. For this reason, it is useful in fireproofing materials and insulation, especially in walls and ceilings. The substance separates into small fibers and can be woven into a fabric. It cannot be easily destroyed.

Exposure to high levels of airborne asbestos fibers is believed to cause a lung disease called asbestosis, which is chronic and incurable. It causes worsening shortness of breath. Asbestos exposure can also lead to mesothelioma, a deadly and rare cancer of the membranes lining the chest and abdomen.

An estimated 11 million American workers have been exposed to asbestos since World War II. Of those who have died, over one-third had lung cancer, stomach cancer, intestinal cancer, or mesothelioma.

Between 1900 and 1989, over 32 million tons of asbestos were used in America. In 1986, the EPA proposed banning asbestos in roofing, flooring, vinyl tile, cement pipe, and fittings. Substitutes for asbestos could be used in these items.

This ban would prevent thousands of cancer deaths among asbestos workers. The asbestos industry opposes the ban, claiming that their products can be safely used with proper precautions and that the costs of the ban would outweigh the benefits.

Meanwhile, some asbestos sprayed on ceilings and walls in 30,000 American schools is crumbling. This is a threat to 15 million students and 1.4 million teachers. Under current EPA rules, schools are only required to inspect for asbestos and tell the parents if hazards exist. Cleanup costs are estimated at $3 billion. Schools in poor areas cannot afford to clean up asbestos without increased local taxes or government help.

In 1984, Congress set aside $600 million for cleanup of asbestos in schools. But, by 1989, only $100 million had been given to schools. Many schools and other buildings still have asbestos. Asbestos exposure is estimated by the EPA to cause 12,000 cancer cases each year.

CONCLUSIONS

Air quality can be improved, but we must be willing to pay to protect our health. We must also put pressure on political leaders to force them to impose deadlines for achieving air standards.

As the cleanup job goes on, areas that once had the dirtiest air are improving. Yet we are finding toxic airborne chemicals in places where the air was once clean. Some of these chemicals travel in the air, then fall to earth hundreds of miles away in the form of acid rain, the subject of the next chapter.

AN EXPERIMENT

Vaseline and Cardboard

What particles are found in air? To find out, cut sheets of wax paper into squares 3 inches on each side. Using a pencil and metric ruler, divide each sheet into 16 equal-sized squares. Thumbtack each sheet of wax paper to a heavy piece of cardboard. Smear the wax paper with petroleum jelly (Vaseline). These squares will be your collectors. Lay them in several open areas where they will not be disturbed. Mark the location on the back of each cardboard.

After four days, gather the collectors. Do not smudge the coated side. Examine the squares on each collector with a hand lens (magnifying glass). Compare the amount and type of particles found in each square.

What does the number of particles in a square tell you about the amount of air pollution in that location? Compare the particles collected in different locations. How can you explain the differences? What particles can you identify?

Record all your observations in your notebook.

CHAPTER 13:
ACID RAIN— REQUIEM OR RECOVERY?

We are using the sky as a toxic waste dump. The result is acid rain, one of the ways we are quietly changing the face of the world.

HOW DID ACID RAIN BEGIN?

Acid rain began when we discovered how to burn fossil fuels and produce metals such as copper and nickel by smelting sulfide ores. Rising in the smoke of our success are sulfur dioxide and nitrogen oxides. As these gases blow downwind for hundreds of miles, they are changed to sulfuric and nitric acids, and to substances that contain sulfate and nitrate. They sometimes return to the land as dry particles, called *acid deposition*. They can also fall to earth with rain, dew, drizzle, sleet, and snow; this is what we call acid rain.

Industry and transportation seem to be the main sources of acid rain. Most of the sulfur dioxide (65 percent) comes from coal-burning electric power plants, which produce about 20 million tons of it each year. The rest is made by other industries and by cars. In fact, cars produce about half of the nitrogen oxides. Another 30 percent comes from power plants.

During the last several decades, increased burning of coal and oil has polluted the air in parts of western Europe and the United States Midwest. One solution has been to build taller smokestacks, over 1,000 feet. These stacks release the gases higher into the atmosphere so that local air will not be polluted. This causes pollution on a larger scale, however, because air currents carry the gases many miles away.

Another solution has been the scrubbers installed in smokestacks to remove gases such as sulfur and nitrogen oxides as well as small particles from the gases going up the stack. Different manufacturing methods produce different stack gases. So different kinds of scrubbers must be used to remove these materials from stack gases.

Some scrubbers dissolve sulfur dioxide and sulfur trioxide in water. Other scrubbers neutralize acidic oxides as they go up the smokestack or travel through the air. Still other scrubbers gather the small particles from the gases.

HOW IS ACIDITY MEASURED?

What is alkaline? What is acid? Acid chemicals are sour. Alkaline substances are bitter. To measure the acidity or alkalinity of a substance, scientists use the pH, or potential hydrogen, scale. This scale goes from zero to fourteen, and measures the hydrogen ion concentration that makes water acidic. The symbol pH stands for the exponent or potential of hydrogen ions. It is the negative exponent with base 10. Since the pH refers to the negative exponent, the lower the pH, the more acidic the substance. Distilled water has a pH of 7. It is neutral, neither

The pH Scale

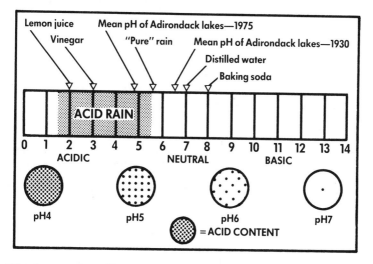

The lower the pH value the higher the acid content. Each full pH unit represents a tenfold change in acidity.

acidic nor alkaline. Values greater than 7 are alkaline; baking soda has a pH of 8.1, and ammonia is pH 11. Values lower than 7 are acidic; lemon juice has a pH of 2.2. The lower the pH of a solution, the more acidic it is.

Carbonic acid is formed by carbon dioxide and water and is present in the atmosphere. It causes normal rainfall to be slightly acidic, with a pH of 5.6.

On the pH scale, each pH unit means a tenfold increase in acidity or alkalinity. That is, a drop in the pH from 5.6 to 4.6 indicates a tenfold increase in acidity. From pH 5.6 to 3.6 is a hundredfold increase in acidity.

WHERE DOES ACID RAIN OCCUR?

In this country, the greatest amounts of acid rain fall in and downwind of Ohio, Indiana, and Illinois, our chief coal-burning states. This area includes most of the northeastern United States. The average pH of rain in most of the Northeast is 4.3, a highly acid rain. Similar levels are found in much of Canada. Highly acidic rainfall has fallen in southeastern states as well. The Southeast is also the region where most toxic metals are found in the soil.

The midwestern states produce 25 percent of all American sulfur oxides and one-sixth of the nitrogen oxides. One possible reason for the amount of acid rain east of those states is the high number of industries and power plants in the Midwest. Unfortunately, they create a

Acid rain in North America

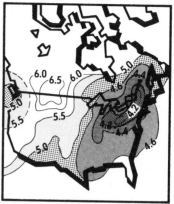

Regions of North America with lakes that are most likely to become acidic

The pH levels of areas that receive acid rain

Legend

SUMMER

WINTER

Legend

NO$_x$

SO$_2$

Major summer and winter paths of storms across the eastern half of the continent

Regions where air contains sulfur dioxide or nitrous oxides

pool of acid air pollution over the entire Northeast. This pool makes it impossible to trace pollution to its source.

EFFECTS OF ACID RAIN

Acid rain can damage both the land and the water. It is most hazardous when it falls on streams and lakes and on thin, sandy soil that is low in lime (calcium carbonate). The damage is greater if the bedrock beneath the soil is granite, and if the lake or stream is highly elevated. Calcium carbonate cancels, or neutralizes, the effects of the acid. Granite lacks calcium carbonate, however, and many lakes at higher elevations have granite beneath them.

Characteristics of soil and water that affect their sensitivity to acid rain.

SLOW ACID BUILDUP	RAPID ACID BUILDUP
1. Alkaline soil	1. Acid soil
2. Thick, loamy soil	2. Thin, sandy soil
3. Limestone (soft) bedrock	3. Granite (hard) bedrock
4. Low elevation	4. High elevation

Areas with limestone bedrock and thick soil will be more alkaline. In such areas, water and land are better able to neutralize the acid in the rain.

Thus, fish are endangered in more than half the lakes and ponds in the Adirondack Mountains. About 600 lakes in that area are now completely without fish. Life is threatened in 48,000 lakes in Ontario, Nova Scotia, and Maine, and in thousands of lakes in Norway and Sweden. These two nations are downwind of polluting industries in western Europe.

Creatures that live in water are also destroyed when surrounding soil reacts with the acid from rain to release aluminum, mercury, nickel, cadmium, and lead salts. These substances leach out of rock formations into the water. Some of these metals cause a mucous coating to cover the gills of fish, suffocating them.

Plants are also affected by acid rain, which reduces the amount of phosphorus in the soil. As less phosphorus runs off from the soil into bodies of water, the number of algae begins to decline. This decline in turn disrupts food chains, since many aquatic animals depend on algae for food and/or shelter.

Acid precipitation can also damage human health. It can cause toxic metals to leach into drinking water, and it can also cause lead and copper from pipes to leach into drinking water. A regular diet of fish taken from threatened lakes may be poisonous if toxic chemicals have biomagnified in the fish. Furthermore, bacterial action on dissolved lead in water produces methyl mercury, which is soluble in fat and thus is biomagnified in the food web. Methyl mercury can damage the brain and nervous system, kidneys, and liver, and also cause birth defects.

Acid rain also destroys works of art. It corrodes marble statues, buildings, grave markers, and monuments, because marble contains calcium carbonate that is dissolved by acid. The estimated cost of such damage in the United

States is $4 billion to $9 billion a year; in Canada it is $2 billion a year.

CONTROLLING ACID RAIN

Various solutions to the acid rain problem have been proposed. Some have been tried. For one thing, new tall smokestacks could be banned. Tighter pollution-control standards could be imposed on old smokestacks, and proper scrubbers could be installed.

The electric power industry says that the cost of scrubbers would be too high. The industry is in favor of nuclear power as an answer to the acid rain problem. But the nuclear power option is twenty-five to fifty times more costly than scrubbers.

Other solutions are: (1) to remove some sulfur from coal before burning it; (2) to tax each ton of sulfur dioxide and nitrogen oxides released from power plants and industries; and (3) to require pollution controls that will remove nitrogen oxides from car exhausts and smokestacks.

Lime has been dumped in some lakes to neutralize the acid. But this process is costly. The neutralizing effect may last several years or only a few months. Dumping of lime may cause some other problems by disrupting the ecosystem and killing more fish. Yet some scientists believe that lime dumping is useful for lakes already affected by acid rain. Fish that have been stocked in limed waters show better growth.

Some species of trout have been developed that are resistant to acid waters. But this, too, is costly. Besides, what is the point? Such a Band-Aid solution does not solve the environmental problem. It creates domesticated fish.

Our country could use low-sulfur fuels like oil, or buy low-sulfur coal from the western states. But we are still too dependent on costly foreign oil. And transporting low-sulfur coal from the West to eastern power plants could be expensive, too.

Many people say that the key to controlling acid rain must be to reduce emissions from fossil-fueled power plants, especially coal-burning plants. One approach combines the use of low-sulfur coal or washed coal with flue-gas desulfurization (FGD).

In FGD, wet limestone is sprayed into the plant's hot exhaust gases. This removes up to 90 percent of the sulfur dioxide. However, the sulfur-ridden waste can be difficult to dispose of. Also, the FGD process does nothing to reduce nitrogen oxide emissions.

There are more efficient methods of burning coal more cleanly. The first is atmospheric fluidized-bed combustion (AFBC). In this method, a bed of crushed coal and limestone is mixed with an upward blast of air. This allows more complete burning of coal at a lower, more even temperature. This, in turn, reduces the formation of nitrogen oxides. The limestone captures the sulfur dioxide.

A second coal-burning method is pressurized fluidized-bed combustion, in which the coal is burned in compressed air.

Almost half of the coal-fired power plants in the United States were built before 1975. They have no emission controls for sulfur and nitrogen oxides. These plants are mainly in the eastern half of the United States. Most of our nation's sulfur emissions come from them.

We could add one or more of these other coal-burning methods to the older power plants. Total emissions of some oxides would be cut in half if this were done.

THE POLITICS OF ACID RAIN

In 1979, the federal government announced plans to build 350 coal-burning power plants before 1995. This plan was intended to make our nation less dependent on foreign oil.

In 1980, the EPA required all new coal-burning plants to use scrubbers in smokestacks. Unfortunately, this rule does not apply to existing power plants. Each of those emits seven times more sulfur dioxide each year than a new plant.

The United States also started a $10-billion plan to convert old oil-burning power plants to coal in order to save oil. Environmental groups expect this change to increase the acid rain problem, especially since existing power plants do not come under the 1980 EPA ruling. The difference in rules for old and new plants gives industry a reason to keep old plants going because they cost less to operate.

In 1980, we signed an agreement with Canada in an attempt to control acid rain. We agreed to take steps to reduce the number of airborne chemicals passing across our boundary and into Canada. Congress passed the Acid Precipitation Act that same year. It called for a $300-million research plan to identify the causes and effects of acid deposition.

In 1987, a report on the findings of this research was published. The quality of the research was good. But many scientists were surprised at the report. It claimed that only a small percentage of lakes in the Northwest were acidified. The report also claimed there was little damage to forests, no crop damage, and no effects of acid rain on human health.

The coal and auto industries agree. They say that there is no acid rain problem. They question the evidence that acid levels are increasing. They say scientists did not monitor acid levels until recently. Thus, how can scientists conclude that levels are rising?

The industries also say some lakes that are close to each other vary widely in acid levels. They say this difference shows that runoff from logging operations may be the chief cause of high acidity. They put pressure on Congress not to repeat the mistake it made in passing the 1970 Clean Air Act, which set standards that could not be reached. Those standards were based on guesses, not on factual evidence.

Scientists agree with industry that there are no quick answers to environmental questions. They agree that more evidence is needed. But they do not think we should wait for that evidence before we act.

For example, they point out that neighboring lakes may have different acid levels because one lake may be sitting on thin soil and granite bedrock, and another may be on thick limestone. This pattern has been found in the Adirondacks.

THE ACID RAIN DEBATE

Not only is this a controversy among government, science, and industry; it is also a debate between different geographic and political regions. The debate is over who will have to pay how much to maintain or improve the environment; and who will have to suffer from the effects of not taking action.

The battle over acid rain has become regional trench warfare. The midwestern states say it is unfair to place tighter pollution controls on their power plants. They claim these controls would put thousands of miners out of work and push up electric-power costs for midwesterners. The controls would also reduce the area's ability to attract new industries and keep old ones. The Midwest questions studies showing its power plants are directly responsible for acid rain.

The northeastern states say power plants in the Midwest could impose tighter controls without losing jobs. They could mix low-sulfur and high-sulfur coal, install scrubbers, and wash their coal better to get more sulfur out before burning it.

Since 1980, the EPA has approved higher sulfur dioxide levels for power plants in seven midwestern states. The northeastern states have challenged these decisions in court. They claim the EPA has violated the Clean Air Act.

But the Midwest argues that northeastern states have relaxed sulfur dioxide levels for power plants inside their own state lines.

Meanwhile, a law has been proposed in Congress. If passed, it would begin a 10-million–ton annual decrease of sulfur dioxide in the thirty-one states east of the Mississippi River. The coal industry has said this law would cause thousands of coal miners in the Appalachian and midwestern coal regions to lose their jobs. Midwestern taxpayers would also have to pay higher electric bills. This increase would pay for the extra pollution controls on their power plants. Many other states would have no such increases. So this law would add more fuel to the fiery debate between the Midwest and the Northeast.

There is a quieter debate going on between Canada and the United States. Canadian officials have urged Congress to control sulfur dioxide pollution. They say our government is not moving fast enough to do that.

American officials say that such a decision must await the results of the ten-year research effort called for in the 1980 Acid Precipitation Act. Some think Canada's real motive is not environmental protection but a wish to sell more of its cheap water power and nuclear power to the United States.

In early 1986, our government did agree with Canada to support a joint $5-billion program to find the most economical way to clean up the burning of coal. Yet at that time the National Academy of Sciences and other scientific organizations agreed that adequate information already existed to start a control effort. The EPA, however, said that more study was needed.

The EPA is supposed to enforce the Clean Air Act. This law does not mention acid rain. But it gives the EPA the power to control sulfur dioxide and nitrogen oxide emissions. The law also controls pollution that crosses state or national boundaries. Yet the EPA claims it has no power to regulate acid rain because the Clean Air Act set limits on sulfur dioxide, not on acids that form from it.

Canada, too, had been criticized for several years for weak regulation of pollutants. Then it became determined to change its ways and set a good example for the United States. In 1985, Canada aimed to cut sulfur dioxide emissions by half within ten years. In 1986, Ontario passed a law requiring coal-fired power plants and copper smelters to cut two-thirds of their sulfur dioxide emissions by 1994. Violation of this law could bring fines of up to $500,000 a day or jail sentences for company officials.

Several states, including New York and Minnesota, also passed acid rain control laws. Between 1970 and 1975, Japan cut its sulfur emissions in half by installing hundreds of scrubbers in coal-fired power plants. West Germany has done the same.

Once started, a federal program for decreasing acid rain in the United States will take at least ten years to achieve its full effect on emissions. Much change will occur in the coal industry. Electric companies will have to study their plans for new plants. People will pay more for electricity. The high-sulfur coal industry may suffer; makers of coal scrubbers may benefit.

According to Management Information Services, an economics research firm in Washington, D.C., the control of acid rain in the United States would save $7.5 billion to

$13 billion per year. There would also be a net gain of 100,000 to 195,000 jobs.

Most miners of high-sulfur coal do not believe these numbers. For those who do, it is little consolation to an unemployed coal miner to know of jobs opening up for electrical engineers or machine toolers to develop scrubbers for smokestacks.

CONCLUSIONS

Acid rain, like many other forms of pollution, causes political and economic disagreements and creates conflicting interests. These conflicts keep us trapped in a downward slide into environmental decay. The acid rain problem also illustrates two dilemmas we face in tackling any environmental problem: (1) how much we must know before we act; and (2) the cost of pollution compared with the cost of controlling it.

Taking action without enough knowledge could lead to catastrophe. But waiting to act until we know everything could also result in tragedy. By the time we understand the problem fully, the damage may be too great to clean up. If we allow the damage to go on, our economic loss will make the cost of the cleanup look like a bargain. We have a choice: win now or lose later. Stated another way, we can pay a lot now or pay more later. Why pay more?

So far, the acid rain story has revealed the EPA as a guardian more of utilities and the coal industry than of the public. In these last years of the twentieth century, the United States faces many complex problems that must be tackled with incomplete knowledge. We cannot keep stalling for time. We need to know that our leaders can solve problems, not just store them for us and our children.

A strong national acid rain control program may not just restore fish and trees. It may also help revive hope and confidence that our leaders can do something about the challenges of today and tomorrow by learning from yesterday's mistakes.

AN EXPERIMENT

Collecting Acid Rain

Get a clean bottle and ask your science teacher for some pH test paper. Put the bottle outdoors when it starts to rain. As soon as an inch of water collects in the bottle, measure the pH. Do this every half-hour until the rain stops. If one inch does not collect, do not take a measurement.

How acid is the rain? Is it more acid when it first starts than it is later on? Why or why not?

CHAPTER 14:
WHAT YOU CAN DO

After reading about the many problems hazardous substances cause in our environment, you may feel that solutions are impossible. You may feel that such problems are best left to the experts, that technology and science will always save us.

But we have seen that some technological solutions just create new problems. For instance, a farmer can increase production by using pesticides, but the pesticides may contaminate foods and may even poison harmless creatures.

We have also seen that the technical experts do not always agree on what limits of chemicals are safe to live with. Citizens in a democracy must accept the responsibility of establishing safe standards for hazardous substances. Only society can decide if certain levels of disease are acceptably small, or if the cost of a control measure is worth the burden it will impose on taxpayers.

ENVIRONMENTAL ATTITUDES

But environmental decisions must be intelligent. We should think about our present attitudes toward nature and one another. Take some time to analyze your own attitude toward our use of the earth's resources.

You have seen that scientists, industry, and government have all contributed to our toxic mess. Consider scientists. Those who work for the chemical industry often support it. They may say, for instance, that the hazards of organic chemicals have been blown out of proportion. Industry has its own interests to pursue. Nearly all hazardous substances result from industrial activities. Industry has caused a massive pollution with its careless disposal methods.

Government action against careless disposal has been slow and inconsistent. State and federal laws regulating hazardous substances were few until a short time ago, so unsafe dumping of waste was legal for a long time. Such laws get passed slowly even today, and many of them are not enforced.

The public must play an important role in solving this problem. People often blame science, industry, and government for pollution. But what about the public itself? All opinion polls show that we want to be rid of hazardous waste. Yet we do not want plants near us that treat such waste. Nor do we want landfills in our backyards. Nor do we wish to give up all those chemicals that make our lives easier, even though their production creates hazardous compounds. Doesn't our indecision make us part of the problem?

These mixed signals show that many people do not know how to judge possible solutions to an environmental problem. Does one approach really solve it? Can it cause new problems? Is there a better way to approach it?

Crucial decisions must be made. They should not be made only by science, industry, and government. They should be made by informed people after hearing all sides of the issues.

You are a student now, but you will soon be a taxpayer and a voter. This is the time you should begin to get involved in the political process. Your decisions will depend partly on whom you believe. This does not mean you should listen only to those who represent science, industry, and government. People who work in other areas may come up with better solutions. The best way to learn is to listen to many viewpoints and not rely on specialists alone.

Good sources of information on environmental issues include the magazines listed in Appendix 3. Each magazine is published by a club or organization. Write to some of these organizations and ask for further information. Your school library or science teacher may have copies of science magazines that contain articles on hazardous substances. Some of these magazines are also listed in Sources at the back of this book.

Regardless of whom you listen to, you must be willing to weigh the benefits of environmental actions against their risks. For instance, you may be willing to risk some long-term effects of one insecticide that is used to save lives threatened by malaria; or another one used to increase food production in poor nations. But you need to ask if such uses may increase our risk of chemically caused cancer.

Thus, two elements are important as you look at solutions to environmental problems: your trust in technology and people, and your ability to weigh risks against benefits.

Political action will be needed to solve our environment's problems. But several things keep people from becoming more active, outspoken citizens whenever environmental crises occur.

First, people are uncertain about how dangerous the environmental crisis really is. They are unwilling to believe that terrible things can happen. This is a natural reaction, especially when experts disagree about the dangers. But these uncertainties can become an excuse for not taking action.

Another barrier to action is people's belief that it will be easier to adapt to the crisis than to prevent it in the first place. There is one problem with this attitude: environmental change could come so fast that adaptation will be almost impossible.

The lack of awareness among the peoples of the world about the environmental crisis also prevents effective action. Most political leaders, let alone their public, are unaware of what is happening. That must be changed.

Finally, the knowledge that solutions to our environmental problems will be difficult discourages too many people. They believe their efforts will bring no change, so why bother?

These attitudes must be changed before the political system will take action. The role of leadership is important in spreading awareness and in giving us a vision of the future we want to create, as well as a picture of the nightmare we must avoid.

We are at an environmental turning point. Is the destruction of one football-field's worth of rain forest every second enough to make us act? Would we react if a giant alien from space were tromping across the rain forest with feet the size of a football field? At least, perhaps then we would pay attention.

Right now, the political and corporate systems have many short-sighted policies at the expense of far-sighted ones. Our world leaders and company executives do things to give their nations and companies an advantage. But their actions are not designed to help the environment.

By the same token, too many world leaders prepare for global war rather than peacetime cooperative efforts to save the world from environmental destruction. They and we need to examine long-term solutions to our environmental problems.

EXAMINING SPECIFIC SOLUTIONS

The following questions are meant to help you understand and evaluate specific solutions. They may help you prevent environmental problems from developing.

1. Is this a technical solution added on to a current technology? (For example, adding scrubbers to coal-fired power plants to remove sulfur oxides.) Will it solve the problem? Will it cause new technical, economic, or social problems? Could another technology be used instead? Could we do without the technology that causes the problem? Or could we do with less of it?

2. Is the solution another form of technology? (For instance, replacing coal-fired power plants with nuclear power plants to eliminate sulfur oxides.) Will it solve the problem? Will it cause new problems? Could we do without the technology that caused the problem in the first place? Or could we do with less?

3. Is this a nontechnological solution? (For instance, a gasoline tax to encourage people to use their cars less, thus saving fuel and decreasing the number of airborne chemicals.) Will this work? Is it politically acceptable to most people? Is it economically acceptable? Is the cost reasonable when compared to the benefits? Is it socially acceptable? Who will gain and who will lose if it is put into effect?

Examine all the solutions to environmental problems with these questions in mind. You may decide that some are good solutions and others are not.

ENVIRONMENTAL ACTION

What do you do when you have come to a decision? How do you put what you have learned into practice? Here are several ways to take action against pollution:

1. Become more sensitive to your environment. Look around; compare what is with what could and should be. What things around you really improve the quality of your life? What are your environmental bad habits?

2. Become more informed about environmental problems. Don't rely on technology to save you.

3. Choose a simpler life-style. Go on an energy diet. For every high-energy appliance you use (such as an air conditioner), give up another. Where possible, use low technology in place of high technology. Try to influence your family's energy use. Walk or use a bicycle instead of a car. Bicycle travel is cheaper. It is also more fun as you learn how to break through the technological film that separates many of us from nature. It also keeps you healthier.

4. Remember that a clean environment begins at home. Change your own living patterns before you try to change those of others. Reduce your production of chemical waste.

5. Begin to make others aware of workable solutions. For every environmental action you decide to take, convince two others to do the same thing. Persuade them in turn to convince two others. Start at the individual level and work outward. Join with others who believe in the same things. This is one way to change the world.

6. Become politically active on local and national levels. Start or join an environmental group, and join a national club (see Appendix 3). Become the environmental leader of your school or neighborhood. The environment would also improve if each of us made a yearly donation to an active environmental organization (see Appendix 3). By doing so, you are hiring experts to fight for change on your behalf. Or volunteer to work for a local political candidate who will fight for such change. Write letters to influence people once they are elected (see Appendix 1).

7. Join or write to political action groups to support their work against the big waste-producers. Such groups try to affect the government's position on environmental problems.

An example occurred in Gray, Maine. People there were concerned about possible groundwater contamination. One woman's laundry smelled funny. Another had two children die suddenly. Both women noticed many people with kidney and nervous disorders. They suspected the cause was a chemical dump near their homes.

They and other town residents formed a political action group. This group wrote to the state, requesting that their well water be tested. Trichloroethylene, trichloroethane, acetone, and methyl alcohol were found in the water.

The group then asked the state to close the waste site. At first, the state refused. But the two women kept putting pressure on the state through phone calls and letters. The state finally agreed to shut the site.

But there was some unfinished business. Neighborhood children were playing in the dump. The women asked the state to put a fence around the dump. The state delayed. So the women gave the state a two-week deadline and created a lot of publicity. On the day before the deadline, the state built the fence.

You as a citizen need not sit back and watch hazardous substances build up. You can tell government and industry that you will not let them create lower prices and more jobs at the cost of toxic compounds in your air, water, and land. Don't believe people who say your opinion means nothing because you are too young. People in government and industry do take action when they get numerous letters on a topic.

But they will not respond if they hear no public outcry. They will instead assume they can act (or not act) as they alone see fit.

ENVIRONMENTAL DECISIONS

How you decide to influence environmental progress is up to you. But remember this. Such decisions are being made right now—by politicians, companies, and ordinary citizens. These decisions often involve expert opinions, but experts can only lay out the choices. You must decide how high a price should be paid and who should pay it. You must also decide what benefits you can give up and what risks you are willing to take. No one is more qualified than you are to judge the social, economic, and moral effects of environmental issues. This privilege and this burden are yours in a democracy.

The future will bring new problems. Some are developing now. Others cannot be predicted. Whatever they are, your views will be important, as will your contribution to the political decision-making process. Now is the time for you to begin to examine possible solutions to problems caused by hazardous substances.

ACTIVITIES

1. Geometric Growth

Let's say a person got two others to become more aware of chemical waste problems, and each of them in turn did the same. It would take only twenty-eight such doublings to convince the entire American population.

This is called geometric growth. It works this way: 1,2,4,8,16,32,64,256, and so on. It is different from arithmetic growth, in which each person tells only one other person: 1,2,3,4,5, and so on.

How many triplings would it take to convince the American population if one person told three others, each of whom in turn told three others? You can consult a reference book to find the current population figures.

2. Organizing for Action

You and several other students will choose a dump, one near you if possible. Ask a teacher to act as your advisor. Learn as much as you can about its operation. Find out who owns the land and who is using it. Also find out the names and dangers of any chemicals being dumped there or released into the air through smokestacks or vents.

Find out who is affected by the dump or any contaminated water or air nearby. Look for help from environmental, farm, union, and outdoor sports groups.

Your chief goal is to close the dump. But list other goals your political action group is pursuing. For example, you may want the state water agency to sample the well water or test the air. You may want the health department to poll the neighborhood, asking about medical problems. You may want the state to declare the dump a health hazard. That will make it eligible for cleanup funds.

Your group should meet after school every few days to discuss its progress. But do not discuss your activity with those outside the group. Keep your advisor informed of your activities.

Find out which government agency gave the company permission to dump. Check to see who has the authority to close it down. Write or call those local, state, and federal elected officials who have responsibility for the area.

You can also do this activity as a role-playing exercise. Half the class can play members of local and state agencies and the company's executive board. The other half of the class will be the political action group.

3. A Student Debate

Plan a class debate on one of the issues discussed in this book. In your debate, present as many possible solutions to the problem as you can think of and the pros and cons of each of them. Try to decide the best course of action.

APPENDIX 1:
WRITING EFFECTIVE LETTERS

Do you write to your congressional representatives or senators? Do you state your views on different environmental issues? Do you agree with their views on these issues?

You may be thinking, "What can my one letter do?" But letters that either support or speak against a particular view can slowly build in number. When this happens, elected officials may see that they must vote the way their people want them to vote. Otherwise, they are not likely to be elected again. Below are guidelines that will enable you to write to your elected officials effectively.

A list of the elected federal officials for your state and district is usually available at the local post office or library. Each year, the League of Women Voters prints a pamphlet entitled, "When You Write To Washington," which lists all elected officials and includes a list of all the committees on which they serve. This pamphlet can be obtained from the League of Women Voters, 1730 M Street N.W., Washington, D.C. 20036. Here are some pointers to help you when you write to elected officials:

1. Address the letter properly:

 a. To the President of the United States
 (Telephone, 1-202-456-1414):
  The President
  The White House
  1600 Pennsylvania Avenue N.W.
  Washington, D.C. 20500
  Dear Mr. President:

 b. To your senators
 (Telephone, 1-202-224-3121):
  The Honorable _____
  U.S. Senate
  Washington, D.C. 20510
  Dear Senator _____

 c. To your representative
 (Telephone, 1-202-224-3121):
  The Honorable _____
  U.S. House of Representatives
  Washington, D.C. 20515
  Dear Representative _____

2. Be brief (a page or less), cover only one subject, come quickly to the point, write the letter in your own words, and express your own views. Don't sign and send a form or machine-copied letter. Make the letter personal, and don't say you are writing for some organization unless you are.

3. Identify the law you are writing about by number or name if possible. Ask the representative or senator to support or oppose the proposed law. You can get a copy of any bill or law by writing to the House Document Room, U.S. House of Representatives, Washington, D.C. 20515; or to the Senate Document Room, U.S. Senate, Washington, D.C. 20510.

4. Give specific reasons for your opinion in your letter. If possible, mention the effect of the law on you or others.

5. Be courteous and reasonable in your letter. Don't be rude or make threats. Don't pretend that you have lots of influence.

6. Don't become a constant pen pal. Quality at the right time is what counts, not the number of letters you write.

7. Include your name and return address in your letter.

8. Remember that getting a bill passed is only the first step. Later on, you can write to the federal agency that is supposed to enforce the law.

APPENDIX 2:
FEDERAL LAWS ON HAZARDOUS SUBSTANCES

1. **The Clean Air Act** (1965, 1970, 1977, 1990) governs air quality in America. It gives the EPA authority to set standards for air quality, and to control the release of airborne chemicals from industries, power plants, and cars.

2. **The Federal Water Pollution Control Act** (1972) requires the EPA to set national standards for surface water. It provides money for secondary sewage treatment of surface water.

3. **The Occupational Safety and Health Act** (1972) gives the Occupational Safety and Health Administration the power to set standards for work hazards, including exposure to hazardous chemicals.

4. **The Clean Water Act** (1970, 1977) gives the EPA the power to set standards to limit the pollution of our navigable waters. The law prohibits the release of hazardous substances.

5. The Safe Drinking Water Act (1974, 1977) gives the states and the EPA the power to set national standards for drinking water. The EPA can control toxic chemicals in groundwater.

6. The Ocean Dumping Prohibition Act (1977) set a 1991 deadline to stop dumping sewage sludge in the ocean off the New Jersey shore.

7. The Water Quality Renewal Act (1984) gave New York City until 1987 to clean up the Hudson and East rivers.

8. The Toxic Substances Control Act (1976) empowers the EPA to require the chemical industry to test chemicals and provide safety information before they are sold. Existing chemicals must first be tested so that the EPA can take action if they pose a risk to public health.

9. The Federal Insecticide, Fungicide and Rodenticide Act (1972, 1977) controls the use of pesticides. It requires them to bear a label that provides clear directions for safe use. It permits the EPA to set standards to control how pesticides are used.

10. The Resource Conservation and Recovery Act (1976) is designed to make sure hazardous substances are safely handled, from production to disposal. The EPA can set standards for companies producing, handling, and disposing of toxic wastes.

11. The Comprehensive Environmental Relief, Compensation and Liability Act, known as Superfund (1980) set up a $1.6-billion fund with money set aside by Congress, to be used to clean up the nation's most

hazardous chemical dumps. The government then sues companies for reimbursement as each dump is cleaned up. In 1986 the Senate and House passed new Superfund legislation, which is intended to expand the program.

12. The Low-Level Radioactive Waste Policy Act (1980) holds each state responsible for its own low-level radioactive waste. A state may set up its own dump or join with nearby states to form a regional dump.

13. The Nuclear Waste Policy Act (1982) directs the federal government to start selecting a permanent disposal site for high-level radioactive waste.

14. The Motor Vehicle Air Pollution Control Act (1965) sets national standards for car exhausts.

15. The Acid Precipitation Act (1980) calls for a ten-year research program to identify the causes and effects of acid rain.

APPENDIX 3:
ENVIRONMENTAL AND SCIENCE MAGAZINES, ORGANIZATIONS, AND AGENCIES

American Farmland Trust, 1717 Massachusetts Avenue N.W., Washington, DC 20036.

Audubon, published bimonthly by the National Audubon Society, 950 Third Avenue, New York, NY 10022.

ChemEcology, published bimonthly by the Chemical Manufacturers Association, 2501 M Street N.W., Washington, DC 20037.

Conservation Foundation Letter, published monthly by the Conservation Foundation, 1717 Massachusetts Avenue N.W., Washington, DC 20036.

Defenders of Wildlife, 1244 19th Street N.W., Washington, DC 20036.

Department of Agriculture, 14th Street and Jefferson Drive S.W., Washington, DC 20250.

Department of Energy, Forrestal Building, 1000 Independence Avenue S.W., Washington, DC 20585.

Environment, published monthly by Heldref Publications, 4000 Albemarle Street S.W., Washington, DC 20016.

Environmental Action, published monthly by Environmental Action, Inc., Room 731, 1346 Connecticut Avenue N.W., Washington, DC 20036.

Environmental Defense Fund, 257 Park Avenue South, New York, NY 10010.

Environmental Protection Agency, 401 M Street S.W., Washington, DC 20460.

EPA Journal, published monthly by the Environmental Protection Agency; order from U.S. Government Printing Office, Washington, DC 20420.

The Futurist, published bimonthly by the World Future Society, P.O. Box 19285, Twentieth Street Station, Washington, DC 20036.

Greenpeace U.S.A., 2007 R Street N.W., Washington, DC 20009.

National Parks and Conservation Magazine, published monthly by the National Parks and Conservation Association, 1701 18th Street N.W., Washington, DC 20009.

National Resources Defense Council, Inc., 122 East 42nd Street, New York, NY 10168.

National Solid Waste Management Association, 1730 Rhode Island Avenue N.W., Suite 100, Washington, DC 20036.

National Wildlife, published bimonthly by the National Wildlife Federation, 1412 16th Street N.W., Washington, DC 20036.

New Jersey Hazardous Waste News, published bimonthly by the Association of New Jersey Environmental Commissions, Box 157, Mendham, NJ 07945.

Nuclear Regulatory Commission, 1717 H Street N.W., Washington, DC 20555.

Nuclear Safety, published bimonthly by the U.S. Department of Energy; order from U.S. Government Printing Office, Washington, DC 20402.

Oceanic Society, Stamford Marine Center, Magee Avenue, Stamford, CT 06902.

Rainforest Action Network, 300 Broadway, Suite 28, San Francisco, CA 94133.

Science News, published weekly by Science Service, Inc., 1719 N Street N.W., Washington, DC 20036.

Science World, published biweekly during the school year by Scholastic, Inc., 730 Broadway, New York, NY 10003.

Sierra Club Bulletin, published monthly by the Sierra Club, 520 Bush Street, San Francisco, CA 94108.

Solid Waste Report, published monthly by Business Publishers, Inc., P.O. Box 1067, Blair Station, Silver Spring, MD 20910.

Worldwatch Institute, 1776 Massachusetts Avenue N.W., Washington, DC 20036.

SOURCES

Bergin, Edward J., and Ronald Grandon. *How to Survive in Your Toxic Environment*. New York: Avon, 1984.

Boraiko, Allen A. "The Pesticide Dilemma." *National Geographic* 157, no. 2 (1980): 145–83.

———. "Storing Up Trouble: Hazardous Waste." *National Geographic* 167, no. 3 (1985): 318–51.

Brown, Michael. *Laying Waste: The Poisoning of America by Toxic Chemicals*. New York: Pantheon, 1980.

Canby, Thomas Y. "Our Most Precious Resource: Water." *National Geographic* 158, no. 2 (1980): 144–79.

Epstein, Samuel S., Lester Brown, and Carl Pope. *Hazardous Waste in America*. San Francisco: Sierra Club Books, 1982.

Gardner, Robert. *Water: The Life Sustaining Resource*. New York: Julian Messner, 1982.

Goldfarb, Theodore D. *Taking Sides: Clashing Views on Controversial Environmental Issues*. Guilford, CT: Dushkin, 1983.

Goldin, A. "What to Do about Water." *Science Teacher* 52, no. 1 (1985): 34–37.

Gould, Stanhope, and Brian McTigue. "Radioactive Waste: A Barrel of Trouble." *National Wildlife* 21, no. 3 (1983): 20–23.

Grady, D. "The Dioxin Dilemma." *Discover* 4, no. 5 (1983): 78–84.

Hickman, H. Lanier, Jr. "Why We Have a Hazardous Waste Problem." *EPA Journal* 10, no. 8 (1984): 10–11.

Hogan, Barbara. "A Primer on Groundwater." *Conservationist* 39, no. 3 (1984): 12-21.

Hornblower, Margot. "How Dangerous Is Acid Rain?" *National Wildlife* 21, no. 3 (1983): 4–11.

Houck, Oliver A. "Remember Clean Water?" *National Wildlife* 15, no. 1 (1977): 26–27.

Hunt, Charles B. "Disposal of Radioactive Wastes." *Bulletin of the Atomic Scientists* (April 1984): 44–46.

Keiffer, F. *A Toxic Substances Primer*, LWV 545. League of Women Voters Education Fund, 1730 M Street N.W., Washington, DC 20036. 1979.

Kusinitz, Marc. "Our Poisoned Water—Threat to Life and Health?" *Science World* 39, no. 6 (1982): 4–7.

LaBastille, Anne. "Acid Rain: How Great a Menace?" *National Geographic* 160, no. 5 (1981): 652–80.

Lash, Jonathan, Katherine Gillman, and David Sheridan. *A Season of Spoils*. New York: Pantheon, 1984.

League of Women Voters. *A Hazardous Waste Primer*, LWV 402. League of Women Voters Education Fund, 1730 M Street N.W., Washington, DC 20036. 1980.

_____. *A Nuclear Waste Primer*. League of Women Voters Education Fund, 1730 M Street N.W., Washington, DC 20036. 1980.

Lindholm, Ulf, and Paul Gnirk. *Nuclear Waste Disposal: Can We Rely on Bedrock?* New York: Pergamon Press, 1982.

Maclean, Donald Bruce. *PBB: The Poisoning of Michigan*. New York: Vantage Press, 1978.

Miller, G. Tyler, Jr. *Living in the Environment*, 5th ed. Belmont, CA: Wadsworth, 1988.

Piper, Dennis, and Fred Ladd. "Toxics on Tap." *Sierra* 70, no. 4 (1985): 56–60.

Shapiro, Fred C. *Radwaste: A Reporter's Investigation of a Growing Nuclear Menace.* New York: Random House, 1981.

Van den Bosch, Robert. *The Pesticide Conspiracy.* New York: Doubleday, 1978.

Warner, G. "Low-Level Lowdown." *Sierra* 70, no. 4 (1985): 19–23.

Weir, David, and Mark Schapiro. "The Circle of Poison." *The Nation*, November 15, 1980: 497.

Weiss, Malcolm. *Toxic Waste: Clean-up or Cover-up?* New York: Franklin Watts, 1984.

Wexler, Mark. "Strike Force." *National Wildlife* 23, no. 4 (1985): 38–41.

White, Donald, and Bob Burke. "Choices in Disposal of Hazardous Waste." *EPA Journal* 10, no. 8 (1984): 20–21.

Worth, Julie. "Hazardous Wastes: A Hazard for Our Wildlife." *Conservationist* 39, no. 4 (1985): 42–47.

Zentner, R.D. "Chemical Companies and the Environment." *Ecolibrium* 9, no. 2 (1980): 7–8.

Zipko, Stephen J. "Gauging Student Attitudes toward Wildlife Populations: A Technique for Teachers." *New Jersey Outdoors* 5, no. 5 (1978): 4–25.

INDEX

ABOUT THE AUTHOR

Stephen J. Zipko is a biology teacher at Randolph High School in Randolph, New Jersey. He earned his B.S. degree in biology from Seton Hall University, and his M.S. and Ph.D., both in zoology, from Rutgers University. He has given talks and presented papers at several conventions of professional associations, and has published more than fifty articles in nature magazines and in journals for teachers. He was named an Outstanding Biology Teacher of America in 1977, and in 1978 he received the New Jersey Conservation Teacher of the Year Award. He received the Science Teaching Achievement Recognition Award from the National Science Teachers Association in 1979 and again in 1982. In 1979 he was named an Outstanding Young Man of America by the American Jaycees. In 1989 he received the President's Award from the Alliance for New Jersey Environmental Education for his contributions to environmental issues.